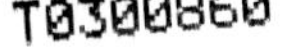

First published in Great Britain in 2014 by Comma Press
www.commapress.co.uk



'Red Lights' first appeared in *Assassination of a Placard* (Beit El Yasmeen, Cairo, 2011). 'Two Men' first appeared in *Searching is a Continuous Rhythm* (Palestinian Writers' Union, Jerusalem, 1997). 'A White Flower for David' first appeared in *The Boy and the Little Sun* (Palestinian Writers' Union, Jerusalem, 1992). 'Dead Numbers' first appeared in *Even the Sea Feels Thirsty Sometimes* (Al Sadaka Forum, Gaza, 2009). 'You and I' first appeared in *Abandonment on the Blackboard* (Egyptian Printing Office, Cairo, 2009). 'Abu Jaber Returns to the Woods' first appeared in *The Mountain Does Not Come* (Dar Al Kattib, Jerusalem, 1980).



A CIP catalogue record of this book is available from the British Library.

ISBN 1905583648
ISBN-13 978 1905583645

The publisher gratefully acknowledges the support of Arts Council England and the Centre for the Advanced Study of the Arabic World (CASAW) who funded two internships with Comma Press which enabled this book to be developed.

This book has been selected to receive financial assistance from English PEN's Writers in Translation programme supported by Bloomberg and Arts Council England. English PEN exists to promote literature and its understanding, uphold writers' freedoms around the world, campaign against the persecution and imprisonment of writers for stating their views, and promote the friendly co-operation of writers and free exchange of ideas. www.englishpen.org

Set in Bembo 11/13 by David Eckersall

# The Book of
# Gaza

Edited by
Atef Abu Saif

With additional editorial support from
Chelsea Milsom and Lauren Pyott.

*To the memory of Eric Page,*
*a true Palestinian.*

# Contents

# Introduction

WITH THE EXCEPTION, perhaps, of Jerusalem, no Palestinian city has been so blessed with media coverage over the last half-century as Gaza. While the city's history dates back to at least 2000 BC, in 1948 Gaza suddenly found itself home to a dense concentration of Palestinians. With the exodus of hundreds of thousands of Palestinian refugees, and with historical Palestinian cities like Yaffa and Akka retreating from centre-stage after the establishment of Israel, Gaza would soon have one of the highest population densities in the world. The city of Gaza became the focal point of a coastal strip that is merely 26 miles long, between three and eight miles wide, and that encompasses several towns and villages, as well as eight of the largest refugee camps in Palestine: Jabaliya, al-Shati, Nuseirat, Bureij, Maghazi, Deir al-Balah, Khan Yunis, and Rafah. Today, over 1.8 million Palestinians live on this small stretch of land, which lies at the heart of one of the greatest conflicts in modern history.

The city of Gaza lies on the south-eastern shore of the Mediterranean Sea. It has been a centre of civilisation since the ancient Canaanite period and throughout the early Islamic period, and played a large role during the time of the British Mandate, which began in 1917. The Shuja'iyya, al-Daraj, Tuffah, and Zeitoun quarters are some of the oldest in the city, while the past 50 years have seen the rise of newer neighbourhoods like Rimal, Tel al-Hawa, Nasser, and Sheikh Radwan. Gaza sits in the north of the coastal strip that bears its name, and in the northern part of the city lies the al-Shati refugee camp, whose houses' windows look directly out over the waves of the sea. The Rafah border crossing became the sole passageway to the outside world in 2000, when Israel banned most Gazan residents from using the Erez checkpoint to cross into Israel. As a traveler, no sooner do you reach Deir al-Balah, halfway down the Strip, than the towering palms loom into view, hinting at the desert not far beyond – a desert that will reach out past the city of Khan Yunis, a few miles away, where the Negev lies to the east, and stretch far beyond the city of Rafah in the south, the last city in Asia, into Egypt.

In 1967, Israel occupied the Gaza Strip and subjected it to military rule, as settlements were built on the Strip, and military checkpoints divided it into smaller pieces. Israel tightened its grip on Palestinians there until December 1987, when the Palestinian Intifada was sparked in the Jabaliya refugee camp in northern Gaza and spread like wildfire. As a result of the Oslo Peace Agreement between Palestine and Israel, Gaza became the political and administrative centre of the Palestinian Authority from 1994 until 2000 (when Arafat moved his headquarters to Ramallah). The city of Gaza witnessed tremendous urban development during the Palestinian Authority's first years, the likes of which it had not seen in the previous century. A multitude of new residential neighbourhoods, public utilities, community organisations, streets, and high-rise buildings were built, and beaches and entertainment centres were set up. Yet the repeated wars and bombings that Israel has launched on the Strip since the Second Intifada began in 2000 have turned back the clock. Countless facilities were destroyed, and a harsh economic blockade was imposed on the Strip, prohibiting people and goods from coming and going. Even fishermen were not spared; for months they were not allowed out on the sea, and when eventually they were, they could venture no further than 1.8 miles from shore. Hospitals, the sick, the poor, and the environment have all suffered the disastrous effects of the blockade.

In writing, as in politics, throughout the past centuries Gaza has always had a central place in the literary life of Palestine. A constellation of Palestine's most important literary figures were born and lived in Gaza, including Imam al-Shafi'i, who was born in the eighth century AD, and who wrote poetry in addition to being one of the most important pillars of Islamic jurisprudence in history, as well as Muin Bseiso and Harun Hashim Rasheed, both born in the first half of the twentieth century. For nearly a century, Palestinian literature has honestly expressed the crisis of the Palestinian people. It has been the faithful scribe of their history, events, and tragedies, of the details of their displacement and refugeedom. Literature has been the living voice of the Palestinian struggle, in the face of being uprooted, displaced, and occupied. From the poems of Mahmoud Darwish, Samih al-Qasim and Muin Bseiso to the stories of Ghassan Kanafani, Emile Habibi and Samira Azzam, Palestinians have also made great contributions to Arabic literature more broadly. Indeed, this literature has not only been a fundamental part of national identity, but helped strengthen it as well; poems are sung and chanted at weddings, in joy and in sorrow, and stories have become part of popular consciousness and wisdom.

With Israel's occupation of Gaza in 1967, most of its writers took refuge outside the Strip. Great poets like Muin Bseiso and Harun Hashim Rasheed, as well as novelists such as Ahmed Omar Shaheen and others left for Egypt and Beirut. Despite restrictions on freedom of expression, the art of the short story attained great popularity during the 1960s, 1970s, and 1980s, and proliferated throughout the Strip. Through the brevity and symbolism of the short story, Gazan writers at times found a way to overcome printing and publishing restrictions imposed by Israeli occupation forces. The Palestinian novel written in Gaza during this period also was characterized by its concision – not exceeding a hundred pages at most, it was an art form perhaps closer to the novella.

Copying and transporting a story to publishing houses in Jerusalem to be printed was no easy task, and so its short length helped facilitate publication. Gaza, as was said in Palestinian circles abroad, became 'the exporter[1] of oranges and short stories'.

During this period, the short story in Gaza was characterized by its focus on national issues and values. It shed light on simple characters, people living in camps and in the neighbourhoods of Gaza City, overcome with hardship and suffering, yet filled with determination and defiance. At the time, most short story writers such as Zaki al 'Ela, Abdallah Tayeh, Ghareeb Asqalani, Subhi Hamdan and Mohammed Ayoub worked in the field of education. They had direct contact with readers, including students and the educated, yet they were also often subjected to harassment by the Israeli authorities. The peculiarities of individuals were glossed over in favour of humanitarian causes; fictional characters were more like representations of particular circumstances, speaking on behalf of society as a whole. Literature had to undertake the role it had aspired to, and it lived up to the task: it created a space for engagement in a society subjected to strict censorship, repressive measures, and with hemmed-in horizons. These were stories of exhausted workers who stood in long queues at the Erez crossing to work in Israel, stories of curfews and cordons imposed on the camps, stories of prisoners' suffering. Gazan writers devoted great attention to stories of challenges, determination, solidarity, and cooperation between people, to stories of the search for work. They wrote of their lived reality, and they did so honestly.

With the end of the 1990s, the presence of a Palestinian political authority, and the emergence of new kinds of power relations within Palestinian society, the range of themes in short fiction expanded to express social conflict and economic problems that people faced, yet the importance of the Palestinian national cause never faded. The setting of short

1. The Arabic word here 'tusaddir' means both 'to export' and 'to publish'.

stories began to take a clearer shape, and the length and themes of the novel also became more consistent. Dialogue in stories became less general, and characters were no longer simply embodiments of grand ideas. Instead, they became more alive; they spoke more passionately about human failings and their own pains and dreams. There was a shift from the public to the private in the structure and themes of short fiction, as well as in the setting, and we began to see more of Gaza's streets, coffee shops, and community organisations.

Young writers grew more attached to their inner worlds as a way of speaking about the world at large. Different themes emerged to express these changes, and instead of writing about the occupation's restrictions, writers turned to themes like self-realisation, critical reflection on the past, the desire to travel, social conflict, love and relationships, and past social constraints that have now disappeared. Writing offered a critical lens on society. With modern tools of communication, the younger generation seems more open to the outside world, and they have begun to speak about themselves more freely. Personal stories and autobiography emerged, as have intellectual stories that reflect a state of anxiety, and attempts to search for one's own answers. In other words, salvation in these stories is a personal matter, in contrast to the heroic, collective liberation for which earlier stories had strived. Even so, the national cause has not faded entirely from the short story's themes. Feelings of disappointment and the failure to achieve one's dreams are what have encouraged this generation to delve into themselves and search for personal salvation.

This book brings together ten short stories by ten short story writers in the Gaza Strip. They represent a range of experiences, a composite reflecting the rich world of fiction in this small spot on the globe, better known for feeding the world's hungry media with a steady stream of headlines. The writings of Abdallah Tayeh, Zaki al 'Ela, and Ghareeb Asqalani represent the generation that founded the short story in Gaza in the 1970s and 1980s. Their stories reflect the reality of the camps in careful detail, revealing people living in destitution, their longing for a better life and their struggles against the occupation to achieve it. In Zaki al 'Ela's story, Abu Jaber represents the archetypal man who withstands pain and torture for the sake of his country, never breaking down in the face of the army's cruelty. Abdallah Tayeh offers a careful portrayal of the state of anxiety and anticipation that his characters live in, and of the unknown but precious future that awaits them – like the contents of the box they keep hidden. Meanwhile, the young Palestinian boy in Ghareeb Asqalani's story chooses not to abandon the human condition when he gives an Israeli soldier a flower in the thought-provoking tale 'A White Flower for David'. Humans cannot forsake their humanity, Asqalani seems to say.

Next come the writings of Talal Abu Shawish, Yusra al Khatib, and myself, who paint a more troubled world, blending the search for lost love with a harsh reality in which mobility is nearly impossible. In my story, searching for a certain place means searching for one's self, just as fleeing from the present means discovering the mistakes of the past. As Talal Abu Shawish shows, thoughts of travel and hopes of expanding one's horizons are starkly reflected in how narrow and cruel reality is – the same reality in which Yusra al Khatib's characters try to find enough room for themselves. There is a great sense of sorrow, disappointment, and defeat in these stories, in contrast to the world of heroism, hopes and dreams that filled the tales of the previous generation, when it was still possible to be a hero.

Quite significantly, women have entered the world of the short story among this new generation of authors. This collection includes four young women writers: some well-established, with a clear presence in Gaza's literary scene, and others who are finding their way in confident strides. Mona Abu Sharekh and Nayrouz Qarmout's writings offer a critical – and one might say, frustrated – engagement with social reality, particularly with regards to the perspectives of women. Najlaa Ataallah's story deals with a harsh reaction to society's constraints, a tale marked by her own personal world, while Asmaa al Ghul explores love that seeks to be freed from the dominance of men and society alike. Their writings illustrate how the range of themes in Gazan short stories have expanded over the last half-century.

This book seeks to paint a portrait of Gaza through the eyes of its writers, as a city different to the one presented in the media. Gaza is a city like all cities by the sea, where people relax on the beach, where the streets have names and the coffee shops their patrons. People love and hate, they are filled with desires and wracked with concerns. They live on a remorseless stretch of land, in a reality that tries to kill their desire to live, yet they do not tire of loving life, as long as there is a way to do so.

Atef Abu Saif,
Gaza, 14 April 2014

*Translated by Elisabeth Jaquette*

Jabaliya
al-Shati
GAZA
NUSEIRAT
Boureij
Maghazi
Deir al-Balah
KHAN YUNIS
RAFAH

# A Journey in the Opposite Direction

## Atef Abu Saif

### Translated by Thomas Aplin

THE FOUR OF them returned disappointed.

Even the god of coincidence could not have so masterfully contrived their unexpected meeting outside that garage in the middle of Rafah. Thin shafts of evening sunlight played across the surface of the road that ran west from the square in the centre of the border-city. Bunches of bananas and dates hung like lost opportunities in front of the large fruit stall on the corner of the square. Honda and Mercedes taxis were lined up beneath a high awning waiting for passengers travelling north; there was nothing south beyond Rafah until the crossing into Egypt. Five drivers waited to load their cars with passengers. At this time, towards the end of the day, there was little traffic and few travellers, as most movement was in the opposite direction, with people returning from work or from visiting friends and relatives in Gaza City. A group of travellers sat in plastic chairs in the little café, behind the cars, sipping hot anise tea. Their voices rose as they debated an issue that appeared to have irritated the café's proprietor. He ground out his cigarette with his foot, exhaling smoke which formed a cloud around his thick moustache - jet black apart from the stray wisps that escaped through it. 'Politics, politics. Enough already!'

The 'café' was really more of a small wooden hut filled

with nargilah pipes, cigarettes and a little fridge stocked with fizzy drinks and juices. There was just enough space for its owner to squeeze inside and make the hot drinks on the little gas stove beside the fridge, or prepare a nargilah pipe before crowning the tobacco with burning coals from the iron brazier outside the hut. Tongues of flame shot up from the brazier like hands, waving to travellers, inviting them to rest a while in this cosy café before continuing on their way. The journey was no more than forty kilometres, but as the longest stretch of coast – which began at Rafah – it was the lengthiest journey any resident of Gaza could make. He placed a nargilah pipe in front of a customer and wiped down the little tables that were packed around the hut and in the narrow corridors between the parked cars, which sat like idols beneath the awning.

The electronics stores, the shwarma shop, the huge new cafeteria across from the garage... A sense of calm prevailed over all, broken only briefly when a bus dropped off a group of young women returning from a long day of study at their universities in Gaza. A light dusty wind blew, punctuated by occasional gusts of hot air, heavy with the smell of the desert that stretched out beyond the wire border fence to the south. The scene suggested it was the end of an exhausting day for all.

Ramzi parked his little blue car outside the shwarma shop, cutting off the singer playing on cassette before she could complete the first verse of her sad song. He walked over to the little café and pulled out a chair into which he sunk his tired limbs. One of the Hyundais filled up, bringing a smile to the face of its driver, who had been waiting over an hour, calling out for passengers heading north to Gaza. The proprietor, a man of keen judgement, brought Ramzi a nargilah pipe without being asked. Someone sitting at another table might have assumed he was a regular. Ramzi gave the proprietor a look of thanks. The man nodded as he lit a cigarette and asked in a low voice: 'Coffee?'

'Ashab,'[2] replied Ramzi. He inhaled deeply from the nargilah pipe, as though drawing large draughts of rest and calm, something he had not known throughout this pale day, pale like his face was now. The proprietor brought him a cup of the sweet herbal tea; there were sugar granules around the rim. Two middle-aged men sat down at the next table. The smell of tobacco drifted out with the clouds of smoke that left Ramzi's mouth and floated around him, like nebulous thoughts, towards the border where he had spent the entire day. He had waited there, from the early hours of the morning until evening, for the brother he had not seen in twenty years. These years of separation had suddenly been broken by an unexpected phone call from his brother, telling him that he would finally be coming to Gaza, that he could no longer stand living so far from home. Ramzi raised the cup of ashab to his mouth and took his first sip. As he did so his eyes met those of Samir, walking towards him. Samir pulled out a chair and sat down.

They had not seen each other since university ten years ago. The last time they had met was on the day of their final exam, which was held in the huge hall of the old al-Azhar University building. After the exam, they left together and sat on one of the stone benches in the park next to the university. They talked about their hopes and dreams for the future – goals which they would dedicate their lives to achieving. Cars sped along the road in front of the park, cutting through red lights to make way for the procession that bore the body of one of the martyrs from the Shifa Hospital to his home in the Ramal neighbourhood. Voices were raised in anger. Politicians walked among the marchers thronged by guards, photographers and journalists. At the back, women bewailed the young man whom death had snatched away. Ramzi and Samir got up to join the procession, then parted and did not meet again.

All at once, these moments leaped onto the wooden table before them, into the present where none of their

2. A kind of herbal tea.

dreams had been realised, and the fruit of life, whose tree they still climbed, remained mostly unpicked. Two cups of ashab were followed by two cups of coffee and talk that led to yet more talk about dreams, life and plans. But this time, the share of disappointments, defeats and unpicked fruit was greater than it had been ten years ago, when the angry procession had surged through the city streets carrying that guiltless young lad. Then, the flower of youth had been in full bloom, its perfume intoxicating their senses, and glowing brightly, like one of the burning coals on Ramzi's nargilah pipe as he sucked in the tobacco and exhaled a cloud of smoke that swirled up and around their heads.

Samir was returning to Gaza after ten years of estrangement. 'Gaza is nicer from the outside,' he said looking around him as he wiped away the sugar from the rim of his cup and licked his fingers. The years had passed quickly, like the clouds of smoke that blended with the gusts of warm desert air blowing intermittently from the south. He had left to work as an accountant for an investment firm in Dubai. At first the world smiled at him. His new job came with a generous income, which he used to put his brothers through school, build a family home in the camp, pay for his sister's wedding, and buy a piece of land on which to build a beautiful house facing the sea. All this he did without once returning to Gaza. Instead, he sent the money to his brother who took care of things. The idea of returning to Gaza had given him a particular kind of headache, especially with the repeated closure of the only crossing, linking Gaza to the outside world via Egypt. Then there was the difficult journey across the Sinai desert, which he loathed, followed by the hours of waiting at the crossing before he could enter Gaza. Thinking about the return journey was even harder. A traveller had to wait days - even weeks - on the Palestinian side before they could perform the miracle of leaving Gaza. He made do with sending money and gifts, greetings and best wishes over the phone, although after ten years this had no longer been enough. His mother's tears, her imploring and sighing began to keep him awake at night. The old lady, who was in her eighties, had but one dream: to see the family sat around the same table, eating dinner together one last time. But since her eldest son was still in prison, it was a dream that couldn't be realised. Samir's brother had spent twenty years of his existence in there. Every peace agreement had failed to free him, and none of the Monday protests outside the Red Crescent head quarters on Gaza's al-Jala Street had succeeded in opening the cell of the son who was barely twenty when they locked him away.

Yet Samir could not see his mother completely deprived of her dream, so he had decided to return to Gaza and bring the family together, even if it were an incomplete reunion. An old lady, trailed by two children, motioned to the fruit seller to pick her two kilos of bananas. He handed the children a bunch each. The square seemed peaceful as the shadows crept in, enfolding it like a black cloak that had dropped down from the sky.

The café's proprietor, a man in his sixties, removed the coals from Ramzi's nargilah pipe. He blew into the head to expel the smoke trapped inside, and then placed it back on the pipe, before returning the coals. Ramzi laughed and said: 'You made it and then came back!' It was a feeble laugh, since just to think about the future was enough to kill any passing moment of happiness. Often, we must find the courage to accept our reality. Samir nodded as he realised that his reality was already catching up with him and he was barely across the border. Ramzi's brother had not been able to return through the crossing. He had waited three days, only to retrace his steps at the end of each one and spend the night in the little hotel in the Sinai city of Arish. The following morning he would wait again at the barrier on the Egyptian side, where thousands of travellers pushed and shoved as they exited through the iron gate in a surreal, nauseating scene.

After three decades of life in Italy, Ramzi's brother had decided he was tired of living so far from home, and that he wanted to return to Gaza and invest his not insubstantial savings there. One time, he had talked about opening up a furniture factory; another, a building contractors; and a third, a big wholesalers warehouse in the centre of Gaza City. 'This country deserves the wealth of its people more than anywhere else.' Ramzi had no clear recollection of the last time he had seen his brother, which was at the end of the 1970s, before Ramzi had even turned five. He had studied in Cairo and then went to Italy to complete his studies in Milan, but before long, he discovered opportunities in the employment sector that academia could never offer. His father died and was quickly joined by his mother. He did not return to Gaza once during those long years. It was only through technology that Ramzi had come to know his brother's face – through photographs and talking to him over Skype. He felt such joy as he watched his brother's children grow from one photograph to the next.

Ramzi looked at Samir, whose eyes roved around the café. Those difficult moments in which memory catches us unawares... This is exactly what Samir had not wanted to happen, that his mother should die without him having been able to look into her eyes. There are some duties that cannot be neglected. Duties and responsibilities - this was exactly what was weighing him down. Ramzi shook his head, as if to free it of all the thoughts that were crowding his mind, thoughts about his brother who had deprived his own parents of a proper goodbye. His mother had died remembering that rainy March morning when his brother left the house and the Peugot 405 took him through the muddy streets to the border. Right up until the moment of her death, she continued to blindly wave her arm in the air searching to embrace a neck that was not there. Why had he decided to return now? Ramzi smiled as he told Samir he wasn't all that upset when he heard his brother hadn't been able to cross the border. True, Ramzi had wanted him to, but he wasn't the one who mattered; those who really mattered had already passed into the shadow of death.

On the far side of the car park, two young women stood, each leaning against a lamp post. The circular lamps that hung from the posts gave the impression of falling stars. They flickered as though to mirror the fitful thoughts of the women, exhausted after a long day of travel, during which they had failed to cross the border. Everything in Rafah suggests 'border-city', on the edges of which the parameters of things change: from the barbed wire, visible to anyone approaching from the east or south; to the suitcases belonging to travellers coming and going from the direction of the crossing; to the accent of its inhabitants with its Bedouin influence; to the goods smuggled in through the extensive network of tunnels beneath the border area, making the earth as hollow as Swiss cheese; to the last dusty road that separated Asia from Africa, close to the wire border fence with Egypt, where one world ended and another began.

Samah's observations bored her friend, Nadia, who stared along the road that ran west in the direction of the sea, where seagulls flew in the distance, making a journey she herself was unable to take. Nadia had waited more than a month to set foot over the border, and now here she was retracing her steps, having failed, dragging her dead dreams behind her, like the heavy suitcases in which she had packed everything that connected her to Gaza. She had told everyone she was going to begin a new life over there. She even packed the little rug a friend had bought her five years earlier. She had never unrolled it because she wanted to keep it clean and only abroad would she find a home fit for it. She even withheld it from her marital home – the marriage ended in divorce after less than a year. She would picture herself flying on the rug at night, like Aladdin's magic carpet. She loved to imagine Shahrayar telling her stories every night, rather than Shahrazad. The day her divorce came through she felt an enormous sense of freedom. Nadia had suddenly found the man who had offered her life on a golden plate, talking of freedom, equality and how women were half of society, raising his hand to her because she was late making dinner. She ran out of the house and back to her family home, never to return. She divorced him relinquishing all rights except her freedom. Nadia's sadness and the crushing sense of failure and disappointment were of no use to her, so she came back to life. And life opened its arms when she managed to obtain a bursary to study in Greece. She would look out over the sea from her window and imagine the waves carrying her there. It was no great distance, but there was still a long way to go. Tens of thousands of citizens were vying to cross the border so it was no mean feat to secure a travel date. The official had finally handed her a piece of paper with the number fifteen written on it, the number of the bus that would carry her. That day she came home with pastries and pizza for everyone. Her joy was indescribable. Finally, her dreams were about to become a reality. Finally, she would find a home whose floor her little rug could embrace. She looked out the window at the sea. The fishing boats were ploughing the waves as they sailed west in search of a catch. When darkness fell, the boats turned on their lamps to attract the fish up from the sea's depths. The ships formed an illuminated road that stretched far out into the sea. It was this same road that she dreamed of following all the way to Greece. She closed her eyes and imagined herself running along the illuminated sea road.

Nadia's shoes scraped on the tarmac. The noise of each footstep on that bright sea road equalled the racket Samah was making as she dragged the suitcases to the side of the road, away from the traffic. She opened her eyes. She had no idea why Samah was so insistent they wait for her brother to come from Gaza to pick them up; they had been waiting for him over half an hour now. The situation came to a head when Samah's mobile phone rang and she learned from her brother that his car had broken down close to the Wadi Gaza

Bridge. A feral rage contorted their faces. Samah took out a cigarette and lit it with a match, which she stamped out angrily. Everyone in the garage turned to look at the young woman with the long black hair in the red jacket, exhaling white smoke.

For Samah too, this had been her one chance to begin a new life. The international organisation in Gaza where she had worked for almost seven years, had offered her the opportunity to transfer to its Beirut branch. Gaza was hard on her. It was hard on her constantly. Her father was fairly well-off and owned a big shop in the Ramal neighbourhood, which sold imported electrical appliances. Of all his worldly possessions, his two children were everything, and Samah was his only daughter. But Gaza was hard on her. It was surprising how quickly her long hair had managed to become a family issue – the key to her honour – after she refused to imprison it under a head cover. The family disapproved of Samah's decision not to cover her hair. Her father stubbed out his cigarette in the ashtray saying, 'The girl is free.' At first it cost him the enmity of his brothers, although they soon made up with him - albeit grudgingly. The difficulties, setbacks, and ugly remarks mouthed by old and young men alike; none of these prevented the young woman from living her life. She went to university and graduated, and all her would-be suitors went home disappointed. At night her mother would whisper to her that life is like a train journey and the first stop is marriage. A girl can't go without a husband forever. In the end, she will have to accept one of her suitors. But the one and only love story of her life was wrapped in a thin tissue of amnesia.

Before long, this tissue would be shredded and its pieces scattered by the hot gusts of wind blowing in from the south, from the direction of the desert.

Ramzi looked in the direction of the young women at the same time as everyone else. His eyes met Samah's in a coincidence that not even the Book of Wishes could have reasonably included. He flinched, as though scalded, and motioned to Samir, as Samah and Nadia began to drag their suitcases towards the little café. Tales of love gathered around the small wooden table that stood between four chairs. There sat the four friends of yesterday as if in solemn celebration, reviving the past from the ashes of the previous ten years. The past on which the dust of forgetting had settled, and whose cry had been lost in the shuffle of life.

Would anyone believe there was a love story around this table? In fact, there were two old love stories here, stirring from the slumber of days past.

Indeed, if someone were to guess that Samah's one and only true romance was with Ramzi, then they would not be wrong. This shy young man had fallen in love with such a bold young woman. On their first date at Café Delice, close to the Rashad Shawa Cultural Centre, he had hidden behind the pages of the Al-Ayam newspaper to avoid looking into her eyes. Five minutes passed before she gave him a sharp jab with her heel: 'Did you bring me here just so I could watch you read the newspaper?!' But love has ways and arts that not even the most adept storyteller could imagine. For four years the flame of love had burned in their hearts, until it encountered the fierce opposition of Samah's family. Her father went crazy when he learned that she wanted to marry a poor young man who lived in a two-room house in the al-Shati refugee camp. This time he had no choice but to stand in his daughter's way. He told her that he'd stood up to the family before when she decided not to cover her hair, but this time he'd stand up to the whole world if it meant his daughter would have the life she deserved. No amount of crying or pleading would change his mind. She had remained unmarried, not through lack of desire or because she wanted to miss the stop her mother had talked of, but because of family pressure. One day she screamed at her parents: 'I'm not marrying anyone I don't love.' Then she broke down on the sofa, like the sun falling behind the shadows of the sea. Those ten years were hard, like Gaza, and continued to haunt every step she took and every word she said. And here she was now, a candle whose flame was being rekindled before the storm of glances she and Ramzi exchanged the moment she sat down at the table.

Their final meeting had been at Café Delice, the same café that had once brought them together, as though there were a dialectical relationship between the beginning and the end. They exchanged few words. This time she did not jab him with her heel as he turned the pages of the newspaper, instead she wiped the trace of tears from her cheeks, knowing this would be the last time she saw him. Ramzi left Café Delice and walked aimlessly along Omar Mukhtar Street, going east until he reached al-Saha Square. The phoenix sculpture that stood in the middle of the square seemed listless, too weak to rise from the ashes. A carob vendor carried a large steel canteen on his back and on his belt he wore a brass holder into which plastic cups were tightly packed. Ramzi asked him for a chilled cup. Night came as he wandered the streets. He had no idea how he had managed to walk all this distance to his little house in al-Shati camp. That night Ramzi had imagined it was raining, and he awoke terrified. The moon was hidden behind the tall cypresses that stood at the back of the house from where they overlooked the sea.

Samir laid the nargilah pipe across his knees, unable to believe that the wheel of time could turn in reverse. A love story he had never spoken of was now being revived. He had been smitten with Nadia and her eyes had revealed the love hidden in their depths. They had met only on the stairs or in the park in front of the university; there had been no other contact between them.

Except, this is not entirely true. Samir and Nadia were born and raised on the same alley, in the same camp. As children, they would play together in the streets, or in the sand of the nearby beach. But one day, Nadia just disappeared.

She no longer came out, other than to travel to and from school. Her breasts swelled and her body suddenly matured. Almost over night she was forbidden from playing with boys. At first she didn't understand, but the scoldings soon made the matter clear enough. The little girl became a woman before her time; she began to dress in women's clothes and to behave like them.

Time passed, and when time passes we do not notice the thick dust that its wheels throw up because we are too preoccupied with our many pains and joys. Their eyes met at university as he was coming down the stairs and she was going up. There is a certain something in the eyes that cannot be mistaken. They paused and looked at each other before their lips curled into smiles that brought back the past. Then they went their separate ways. Those looks and smiles had been the only form of communication between them, even when they would meet in the taxi on the way to university.

This same routine would play out around the small table in the Rafah garage café, that evening on which the moon climbed the sky, like a beauty spot on the cheek of a young girl. Samir and Nadia exchanged glances, neither saying a word. The past was climbing the edges of the tabletop, to sit in its middle while they stared at it, incredulous at its tenacity. The scene appeared somehow strange to the café proprietor. That two young men and two young women should sit together, laughing and teasing one another as the smoke of their nargilah pipes blended and billowed above their heads. A passing policeman stroked his thick beard as he pointed out it was forbidden for women to smoke the nargilah pipe. The proprietor laughed and told him to go and tell them himself.

Before the policeman reached them, they stood up from the table together. They dragged their suitcases, like the dreams that burned in their hearts, to Ramzi's car. They got in and headed north to Gaza. The moon followed them in the eastern sky. Orange fields stretched along the road into the distance. Words about 'the past that once was' were softly sung, university stories and moments that shone in memory. Ramzi's phone rang to tell him his brother had decided to return to Italy; it was difficult to enter Gaza and leaving even more so. Gaza is just a big prison. Ramzi smiled as he told himself he knew his brother would do this in the end. He had never gone to any great lengths to be with them.

It was as though the past had not died. Samah looked at Ramzi, deep in thought as he stared out at the date palms that lined the road, running parallel to Deir al-Balah city, as though to signal the end of the desert. She felt her heart thumping like it used to. She asked him quietly: 'Are you still angry?' He smiled. At that moment, they realized that neither of them had married. That obstinate love in their hearts was even more stubborn than Gaza. The world and circumstances had changed, but although Ramzi was now director of a branch of the Arab Bank, he had not wanted to marry. It was as though he had wanted to remain true to the beautiful jab he had felt on that first date in Café Delice.

When she noticed the distracted look on Samir's face, Nadia resolved that this time she would take the initiative. But before she could say a word he surprised her, saying: 'Gaza is nice.' He laughed. She laughed with him and they launched into a torrent of conversation, reproaching one another for how, all those years they had just stared like statues, neither saying a word. She told him she had made up her mind to talk to him a thousand times, but that she was always too scared and didn't know why. He admitted that every morning, he would psych himself up to say hello to her, but in the end he had always failed.

The moon escorted them, as though to protect them from the phantoms of the night. The lights of Gaza city began to appear from behind the orange fields when Ramzi suddenly cried, 'The moon has disappeared!'

Samah laughed: 'Who's stolen the moon!'

Ramzi stopped the car and the four of them got out,

drunk on the beauty of the moment as they searched the sky for the moon. It was veiled behind a bank of cloud that was gathering above Gaza. Samir suggested that perhaps the moon had decided to remain back, in Rafah. 'I saw it just a short while ago, near Deir al-Balah behind the date palms.'

'It must have returned. We have to follow it,' said Nadia. They felt as though they were on some sacred mission to find the moon. Ramzi turned the steering wheel to head south, back towards Rafah, in search of the moon. Their eyes sought it out between the clouds, behind the trees, together, in that shared moment.

The road was dark, except when they reached a crossroads or where it branched off towards a town or camp. Stories of the past dropped like cherries into the bowl of their conversation. Now and then they would peer through the windows looking for the moon. They reached Rafah. All was still. There was no traffic except for the odd car. The garage was almost deserted. The café proprietor was enjoying his end-of-day break. Sat in a straw chair at the back of the cafe, he lit his nargilah pipe and continued his vigil over the square and the roads leading off it. They got out in the middle of it and looked up to where the moon appeared as it feebly made its way through the clouds that were trying to swallow it up. They laughed loudly, drawing the attention of the café proprietor whose lips burst into a smile his thick moustache could not hide, revealing his teeth, stained a light yellow. They piled back into the car to return to Gaza, since the moon would remain here, in Rafah. They shrugged their shoulders as they gazed at the black clouds, which began to skid across the sky.

The little car sped merrily along the road, a blue flower dancing across the horizon, buzzing with life, talk and laughter. But then the clouds burst with heavy rain, and the evening breeze turned into a fierce wind that shook the orange trees and the date palms. The road became increasingly difficult as water began to collect at its sides and flood the intersections. Anxiety found its way into their laughter and they became tense as they stared out the windows. This time the lights of Gaza City did not appear from behind the orange fields. The going was slow and the road treacherously slippery… As they approached the big bridge over Wadi Gaza, the road got busier and busier until the traffic ground to a halt. The water from the valley had spilled over onto the road and the bridge was impassable. They stopped the car, got out and stood in the rain, looking at the water that flowed from the valley and out towards the sea. By now the road had become a rushing torrent making it impossible to go on.

They stood by the car in the pouring rain, taking in the scene, which looked like a photographic negative: the submerged road, the heaving valley, and the city enshrouded by cloud. The four of them stood in disbelief, giving the impression of scarecrows or ships' masts sunk at harbour. Then together they burst out laughing. The wind carried their laughter far away, across the frothy, churning water to the heart of the sea.

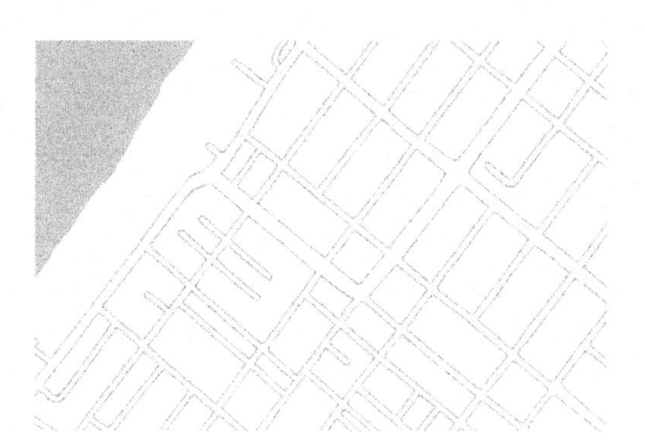

# The Sea Cloak

## Nayrouz Qarmout

### Translated by Charis Bredin

ONCE AGAIN, SHE retreated into the past, to a sprawling camp buzzing with children playing marbles and forming teams for a game of 'Jews and Arabs'. She saw herself aged ten, wearing a short dress and skipping with a group of girls in a sandy alleyway shadowed by sheets of corrugated iron. She dropped the rope abruptly as a little boy snatched a butterfly clip from her hair and ran off with it. She raced after him. Her shoes flew from her small feet but she kept running, oblivious to everything except the sand on the ground that soon carried her to a pathway littered with stones. She tripped and fell. Her dress was stained with dirt but she simply shook the dust from it and ran angrily on.

'Give it back!'

'Got to catch me first!' he called behind him.

They soon grew tired and stopped beneath a large old tree. She leaned against it, grateful for the wide, leafy shade of its foliage. The boy smiled and offered her the clip.

'It looks nice in your hair,' he mumbled bashfully.

Despite her anger, a great wave of happiness engulfed her. She didn't know why, nor did she understand the childish emotions making her heart pound wildly as she struggled to catch her breath. Then suddenly her brother was before them, throwing a wild punch at the boy who immediately threw one back. He had appeared as though from nowhere on the sandy path where they were standing beneath the tree. He punched the boy again. She began to cry and he grabbed her by the arm and dragged her home. On the way he called her a 'hussy', a word she did not understand.

They reached home and her brother went straight to their parents.

'She was with the boy from next door.'

The words struck like lightning bolts. Her father gave her a slap across the cheek that she would remember for the rest of her life. Her mother grabbed a handful of her hair and dragged her away.

'I'll sort her out,' she called to her husband.

'That's the last time you're going out on the streets,' she screamed at her, once they had left the room. 'No more games. You're a grown-up now, not a little girl. Go and look at yourself in the mirror. Take your sister's scarf and wrap your hair in it. I've had enough of these girls and their modern ways!'

She could still hear herself weeping, and feel her hands probing her body, searching for parts that had begun to grow, parts she had previously only known about from her mother.

But all that was in the past. Now was another time.

The walls were suffocating, constricting the cramped house. There was no refreshing breeze and the air was brutally hot. Her father was sweating.

'Where are you all?' he called to her mother. 'Aren't you dressed yet? Hurry up! It's already late and you're still getting ready.'

Her mother continued seasoning the fish while chaos reigned in the adjoining bedrooms. As usual, they had stayed up late on Thursday when her daughters and their children had arrived to spend the weekend with her.

'Stop getting in my way, both of you!' she yelled at the children. 'Go to your mothers and let me finish what I'm doing! And haven't you lot finished dressing and undressing yet? Will one of you please go and see your father? Ugh... these girls will be the death of me!'

She was alone in her bedroom, emptying the contents of her wardrobe onto the bed and trying on one piece of clothing after another. She pulled one on, examined herself then pulled it off again, already reaching for the next. Outfit after outfit and nothing seemed to suit her.

'God I'm fed up,' she murmured to herself. 'It's so hot I feel like I'm melting. The sea looks beautiful though... If only I could chuck these stuffy clothes and have a cold bath.'

She left the room and slouched wearily to the kitchen in search of her mother.

'I've no idea what to wear, so how am I supposed to go to the beach?'

Her mother hurriedly finished what she was doing, her face shiny with sweat. Without looking at her daughter, she tied her scarf into a knot around her head.

'My head's about to explode! Go and take your anger out on someone else... and wear whatever you want to wear!'

Her frustration grew. She felt heat rise within her, even more suffocating than the surrounding air. She watched her mother with a mixture of pity and anger.

'Who am I supposed to go to? You all say the same thing. None of my sisters are free.'

'What did I just tell you? No more complaining, I'm sick of hearing about clothes. Don't ruin the day please, just behave. Moments like these don't come along very often, my dear, so don't let them slip away when they do!'

'Fine. Do you need any help?'

'No, just go and get ready.'

They all managed to squeeze onto the bus and prepared to greet the sea. They had not visited it in some time and each was hoping it would restore fond memories, and bring them an even more glorious day.

Brightly coloured kites danced through the air like little rainbows that, mingling with rays of sunshine, glowed alternately on the foam and the sand.

A strong breeze gusted through the humid air, laden with an array of scents, from sweetcorn to potatoes roasting on burning embers. It was a wonderful scene. Sizzling steam rose from carts displaying pistachios and roasted seeds, each one adorned with twinkling lights like a carnival float. And once your tongue had tired of their burning heat, another line of cheerful stalls stood in wait, offering ice cream of all colours and flavours. How good it tasted as you strolled along the beachfront, the breeze caressing your body and the cool taste refreshing your soul!

The beach was packed with tents and small sunshades cobbled together from planks of wood and palm fronds that wafted a cool breeze over those sitting beneath: the lovers and dreamers, yearning for a day that would steal them away from the troubles of existence. Warm light filtered through the fronds, crisscrossing the sand and filling them with hope. As the fronds swayed, bells chimed softly, tickling their ears.

Gaza's coastline is not clean. Everything is scattered about in disarray. The sand is littered with rubbish and tents dot the beach like bales of hay, where dreaming souls shelter, conversing with their most intimate imaginings. That is just the way Gaza is: a young girl yet to learn the art of elegance. A young girl who has not yet developed her own scent and is still, willingly or not, perfumed by all around her.

The family chose a tent which they soon filled with laughter, chatting happily about the day ahead. They were all in search of memories, contemplating the waves as they surged tirelessly towards the shore, awakening within them nostalgia, hope, and a sense of loss before the great cloak of the sea.

Her father did not know how to swim. He bobbed up and down in the water, relying on his height as he struggled forward before returning to the shore where he sat contemplating the water in such profound silence that everyone knew he had drifted away to a sea far from the one before them. Their mother, meanwhile, busied herself arranging the tent, keeping an anxious eye on the salad that she had just taken from her bag, fearing it would be ruined by the sandy breeze. She was preparing their lunchtime festivities, arranging the table just as it would be at home. It was only when she sat down that she realised how tired she was. During all this, her daughter sat quietly, contemplating her parents.

Then there was Grandma, her embroidered dress fluttering in the breeze. She was chuckling away, an old cigarette balanced between her lips as she puffed out smoke and crooned melancholy folk songs of old. Every now and then, she glanced furtively at her sulky granddaughter.

'Go and have a swim, dear. I'd come with you if I could.'

'On my own?'

'Don't you have a pair of legs?'

'Yes.'

'Go on, before it gets chilly.'

'Ok, I'm going.'

Her sisters were full of laughter, winking cheekily at one another as they discussed their various acquaintances.

'God forgive us all this nattering; it's just a bit of fun!' they spontaneously declared after every round of gossip.

She smiled at her sisters' and grandmother's words, rising quietly to her feet and walking towards the sea.

Passing her brothers, who were grilling fish on the barbecue, she vaguely registered their loud discussions, alternating between politics, memories of the war and intifada, and mockery of their current situation. Vapour and ash from the nargilah danced into the air along with their laughter.

None of them noticed her as she walked through the smoke. It was as though the sea had cast a spell over her, making her invisible to those around her and carrying her like a bride on her wedding day.

She passed a boy of seven, waiting for waves at the shoreline and leaping joyfully as they washed forward. He was soaked and his trousers were slipping down as he and his brother chased one another around, tossing sand and shells back and forth. Their eyes shone with the freshness of youth. They were quick to anger and quicker yet to make up and return to their game. She smiled at them, patting their heads and continuing on her way.

Another boy of four was running around naked, rejoicing in the freedom of his childhood as he flew back to his mother, anxiously awaiting his return from the water. He threw himself into her arms, seeking protection in her warmth from the secrets of the sea that his four short years had failed to comprehend.

Nearby, a group of young men were throwing cards onto the sand, each with the confident certainty of victory. They didn't have a screen to protect them from the blazing sun and their backs were already burning.

One of them twisted round to watch her as she walked past, calling out a chat-up line from where he sat, cards still in hand.

A short distance away, a donkey was immersed in the water, washing away the hardships of a day spent lugging around cartloads of people. It was laughable. Even the donkey had its own place on the beach and in the sea, splashing about in the salty water like everyone else.

Another couple of children were trying to choose which colour of Slush Puppy to dye their lips with, arguing over who would have the red and who the yellow. They were both wearing shirt and trousers and both soaked to the skin. The vendor, meanwhile, sitting behind his simple little cart, was chuckling into his thick white beard, muttering silent wishes and prayers, all swallowed up in the depths of the sea.

At another stall, a young teenager, still clinging to

childhood, hurried forward to buy some lupin beans. He began to strip their skins, chucking them around him in the pervasive chaos of early teenage years. His eyes were bashful and he avoided everyone's gaze, too shy to swim with girls and longing for another sea that would carry him – and his lupin skins – off to some anonymous location. Nearby, the scents of tea and cardamom-infused coffee were wafting from hot coals as an old man recounted tales of the country's history and wars, and of friends long gone.

Behind him, two high-spirited youths were roaring up the path on a motorcycle, carried forward by blaring music and vying with the wind as it gusted in the opposite direction. Their hair was styled into what looked like miniature Eiffel Towers on top of their heads, while their minds remained firmly rooted in the Middle Ages, as they ogled and wolf-whistled at every veiled girl in sight, revelling in their virility. But a towering policeman soon went to block their path, and the motorcycle squealed to a halt, the young men tumbling to the ground and their protests fading amidst the girls' laughter.

'Leave them be. They're happy!' a passer-by smiled to the policeman, walking around the prostrate figures.

The flirtatious attentions of young men on the beach varied from the original and witty to the downright harassing but, in spite of their rowdiness, they added to the warm, festive atmosphere, delighting in all those around them.

But she was oblivious to the surrounding bustle, pursuing her elusive memories as they led towards the sea. The noise of the past would grant her no respite. Her black dress rustled in the breeze and her headscarf fluttered a greeting to the seagulls. With every step that carried her closer to the water, she heard what sounded like the neighing of horses, growing steadily louder inside her.

She drifted forward, carried like a mermaid by the breeze, her thoughts entirely immersed in the waves before her. Time was stealing her steps away, and the sea, without her realising, had already snuck into her memory.

Between the fragrant scent of nostalgia and that of the sea, memories crashed together in her mind as waves surged towards her. She felt the sting of sand biting at her soft skin and longed to escape the black folds of her dress. She sunk her toes into the wet sand, her footprints as light as a butterfly's, dissolving instantly away. She moved forward, fearful of what was to come. Her foot had plunged into an abyss too deep to escape. But she continued, happy to have fallen. Her ivory feet were now soaked and golden grains of sand glistened around them.

She swam further out. Water seeped beneath her clothes until they ballooned around her. She felt an excited tingle that was almost too much to bear. Arousal grew inside her as she continued onwards, oblivious to the seashells cutting the bottom of her feet, making the moment complete with a few drops of female blood. Pain and desire gripped her. Sea foam surrounded her like a bracelet of honey, entwined with froths of whipped candyfloss, its edges gleaming with golden light as it absorbed its nectar from the sun above.

Gazing up at the brilliant white of the sky, she was carried along like an angel of the sea. The cold sea breeze whipped at her skin, sharper even than the biting sand. With eyes shut, she took a deep breath and plunged beneath a wave. It had barely run its course when she already felt an urgent need for air. She surged upwards and her dress billowed out. Tugging it hastily down, she gasped for breath and blushed as she saw the black material clinging to her breasts, displaying her curves to anyone who cared to look. Her cheeks glowed and her dark eyes shone like precious stones, fringed by eyelashes as sharp as arrows. Rays of sun bathed her in a halo of light and her smile filled the shore with boundless joy. She felt air rushing from her and realised she was panting, struggling to catch a single breath.

'I want to keep swimming,' she murmured to herself. 'I want to fly beneath the waves. I want to be as light as a feather on water.'

The sea's symphony, familiar and divine, caressed her ears. Her heart slowed and reached out to the desolate expanse of water. She opened her eyes and was dazzled by golden ripples stretching out as far as she could see. Her body sunk into their warm embrace.

She swam further, propelling herself forward with slender arms and legs as her dress swirled around her, entangling her thighs and restricting their movement. Her scarf, meanwhile, had plastered her hair to her head and felt as though it had been fastened there permanently, covering her eyes.

Her feet no longer touched the ground and she grew afraid, pulling the scarf from her face and turning to look behind her. The people on the beach were tiny dots in the distance and she could barely distinguish them. They too must no longer be able to see her. A strong current was pulling her dress down and she shivered in alarm, sensing her strength fade and fearing she could no longer stay afloat. Her legs felt heavy with the material wrapped tightly around them and she wanted to pull it off but was afraid of her nakedness. She was afraid of death too, and of shame. She loved life and felt suddenly alone. The sky was far above and the sea had grown menacing, its echoing boom resounding in her ears. Tears would not come although she desperately wanted to cry. She gave in to the current but, as she began to go under, a muscular arm suddenly encircled her. She gazed down at it, feeling its strength and warmth.

'I've got you. Hold tight and don't be afraid.'

She grew even more alarmed as scenes from the past flashed before her, urging her to keep far away from any man she did not know. Faint voices rose from the depths. Her mother and father's scolding tones filled her ears. It was her first day of secondary school again, as she proudly stepped out in her new uniform: a child realising she had grown up for the first time, aware of her girlish curves beneath the material and sensing her hair waving in the breeze. Everyone on the street had watched her with an admiration she had not fully comprehended. But she had, at least, understood that she was attractive, and in full possession of herself. Next, she saw a young boy of her own age. He smiled at her and she felt herself smile back. Then there was a path shaded by branches. She and the boy were sheltering beneath a tree as the boy told her how beautiful she was and she felt as though all the birds in the trees were singing for her and her alone. All she could recall was his smile and his broken tooth, both of which she had immediately loved and would never forget. The rest of his features were hazy, fading to nothing as her brother appeared before them, punching the boy and dragging her away by the arm. Then she woke from her reverie, feeling her rescuer tug harder on her arm. They were approaching the shore. She moved feebly and was barely able to draw breath, but she was afraid of him coming any closer. And yet she had liked his arm gripped tightly around her. It gave her a feeling of security she thought she had lost many years ago.

Sunlight dazzled her as she opened her eyes. Tears fell onto her cheeks and lay glistening there. She felt incapable of coherent speech.

'Let me go, I'll carry on by myself.' Garbled words escaped her: 'What will people say?'

The young man smiled in surprise, swimming strongly forward.

'They'll say "look at that handsome young man who's rescued that gorgeous girl."'

'What do you know? Maybe I wanted to die,' she said, overwhelmed by exhaustion.

'No. You got a taste of death so you'd learn to appreciate life. Next time, I'll teach you to swim.'

They lingered in the water, now safe from harm. She glanced into his eyes.

'How?'

'Maybe it was me who was going to give up on life until I saw your eyes,' he said, his words interrupted by the waves washing over them.

They walked the rest of the way to the beach. One of her brothers, a year younger than her, was watching them. In his face, she saw confusion and anger, mingled with affection.

'What happened? Are you OK?' he called, coming towards them.

She remained silent, staring at him wordlessly as she drifted in and out of a daze. The man replied instead.

'She was drowning. But she's fine now, thank God.'

Her brother stepped forward, took his hand, and shook it vigorously.

She remained standing between them. The young man smiled, leaning down to whisper in her ear.

'Didn't I tell you? Life's simpler than you think.'

She gazed at his familiar smile and broken tooth. She remembered her hairclip, the walls of the neighbours' house and the shade of the tree, then felt her heart take flight once more.

She longed for a childhood that had faded away amidst the scolding severity of her family, suddenly afraid of their neighbourhood's scorn.

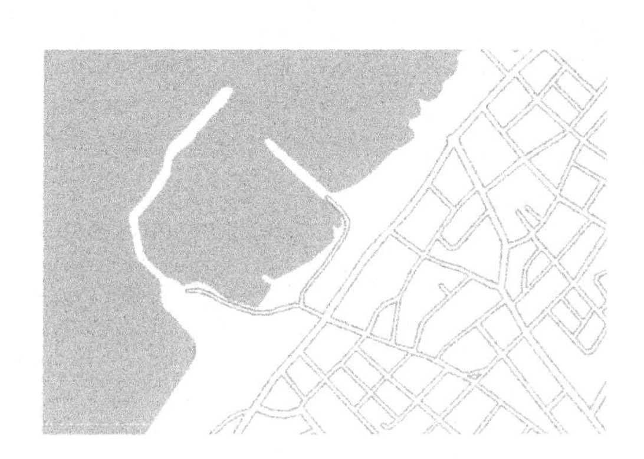

# Red Lights

## Talal Abu Shawish

### Translated by Alice Guthrie

HE REACHES BEHIND him, over the seat, so the passengers next to me in the back of the car can put their fares into his outstretched hand. He carelessly chucks the money down beside him, with a gesture of disgust that I resent. In an attempt to get him talking, I mutter,

'It's a tough situation, but it's temporary...'

'There are more cars than passengers!' he retorts. 'What we take only just covers our fuel costs!'

He falls silent and contemplates me in his rearview mirror for a moment, before continuing bitterly,

'A taxi driver's exactly like a beggar: the only difference between them is that a beggar puts his hand out in front of him, and a driver puts his hand out behind him!'

He stops at a red light near Firas al-Sha'abi market. He sighs heavily, almost violently, with an air of utter exasperation, and begins drumming irritably on the steering wheel with his fingers. A beautiful face approaches. It belongs to a boy who can't be more than nine years old. He's saying something, but so quietly that we can't make out the words through the glass. The driver presses a button to lower the window, and the child's voice fills the car as his hand reaches in, holding out two bars of chocolate.

'Just a shekel! Two for a shekel!'

The driver gives him a shekel and takes only one of the bars. He offers it to us and we all turn it down, so he throws it onto his dashboard and – seeing the lights turn green – clunks the car into gear ready to pull away.

He fiddles with the tape player to get it working, and Oum Kalthoum's voice suddenly soars out. 'Not the right time for you!' he mutters to himself and ejects the tape, turning on the radio. The announcer's quavering voice brings an air of war, raging war, right into the car: siege, assassination, injury, detention.

The driver speeds up, racing to catch the green lights he can see up ahead of us. But before the car reaches them they've changed through yellow to red, and he's forced to stop again. He turns off the radio with an irritable snap and goes back to tapping his tense rhythm on the steering wheel. Another beautiful face draws near. This child is about twelve years old. The driver lets out another infuriated snort and then lowers the window. Once again the sound of a child's voice fills the car – 'Half the price it is in the shops!' – as the little hand thrusts a packet of chewing gum towards us through the window. The driver looks at the passengers' faces in the rearview mirror: none of us move a muscle. He picks up a coin and hands it to the kid, takes the packet of gum from him and lobs it onto the dashboard next to the bar of chocolate. The lights turn green. I suddenly realise I didn't give him my fare when the others did, but I'm reluctant to hand it to him directly – I don't want to see him put his hand out behind him. So I give my money to the passenger sitting next to him in the front, who passes it on. The driver looks at me in the rearview mirror and smiles. We're passing Unknown Soldier Park now, where some mellow faces loll on the green grass, and others exhale nargilah smoke up into the sky above the cafe chairs. Two young men trail along behind a gaggle of careless, coquettish young women, who are wandering around the place in circles. All of them are looking for an escape.

The car turns left towards Rashad al-Shawa Junction. The lights are red, as usual. He pulls up, puts on the handbrake, and reaches for a packet of cigarettes. He opens them and offers them around in case any of us wants to smoke. Once we've all said no, thanking him, he takes out a cigarette and lights it.

A young lad comes over to the car carrying a wet rag. He could just about be over fifteen. He wipes the bonnet quickly then comes around to wipe the wing mirror on the driver's side. The driver takes a long deep breath, looking intently at the lad's face. Then he orders him to stop cleaning the car. The little boy backs away from the car, as the beseeching look in his eyes turns to resignation. The driver beckons him back over and holds out a coin. The boy snatches it in happy disbelief – it's been a long time coming, this sudden payment. He moves off a little way, heading for another car, but our driver calls out to him once again, so he hesitantly comes back over. The driver hands him the chocolate bar and the chewing gum.

'Sell these and keep the money!'

The lights turn green and the car pulls away. It turns left and races off towards al-Azhar University junction, where more red lights await us.

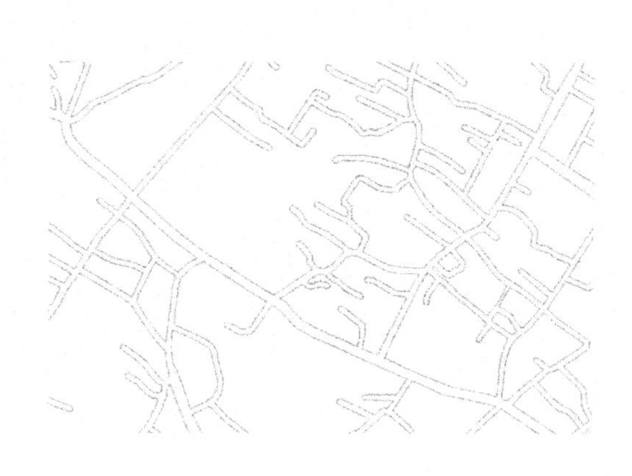

# The Whore of Gaza

## Najlaa Ataallah

### Translated by Sarah Irving

SHE WATCHES THESE shadows forming on the ceiling of her room, the picture emerging from them. In her fantasy, her gaze drifts across the image: those eyes surging with all the pent up desire of a great river in a romantic city like Paris; that nose belonging to a man proud of his origins, rooted in his land; those two cheeks, plump like reddened apples, tempting the onlooker to nibble gently at them; that broad forehead showing beneath the jet-black hair which hangs down to his eyebrows, without overshadowing the radiance of that moon-like face.

She swallows, breaks off her dreamy meanderings and says out loud: 'So, those two cheeks with their ruddy glow, those two cherries spreading over the face, separated by a smile that mingles kindliness and a hunter's killer-instinct, I can only say that I want to bite into them, to see some drops of blood drip from them onto my breast.'

With her eyes she strokes the portraits collected on the walls of her room, all the pictures hanging there of the most handsome men in the world, and raises her eyes to the ceiling: 'You, the bare ceiling, you will stay as you are. My plan for you is to frame the image of a very different man – one who will envelop me with that special love I've heard some men confess to reserve only for their mothers. He will bring together every beauty in his two, gentle hands. What does it mean if the man of my dreams has two soft hands with which to caress a body consumed by the passing years, its details shaped for him alone?' She turns to her own pert breasts and addresses them: 'You're like two beautiful pears, confined and settled in your cradle, waiting for him in your smoothness and softness, for him who loves you...'

She feels a shudder race through her body and quickly pushes her breasts back under her bra and t-shirt, cursing as she does so: 'Shit! Fuck!'

Her hands set to work again, this time sliding down them to her navel, pressing down, as she berates herself: 'How many times did I tell you that this is madness? That dreaming will not draw him any nearer, that he will not be attracted to you!'

She barks at the ceiling, feeling a tingling begin to take hold of her, and struggling with the bed on which she is sprawled. She closes her eyes and tries with all her might to summon the patience of the previous years, to eliminate this image which has taken shape on the ceiling of her room, on this space that mirrors her body – a body that twitches and thrashes angrily, like a chicken that's just been slaughtered, scattering blood like a spray of anger at everything that ever contributed to it being chosen as the victim for today's meal.

The tears that had started welling in her eyes now spill over. She holds her head in her hands, intermittently chewing the fingernails of her right hand and covering her eyes with the left. Her hands move elsewhere, clenching and unclenching, as if performing a massage upon a whole span of her body, every piece of which feels her distress, all of which wants to evoke an idea in her, automatically, joining in the same rhythm of tensing and untensing. Her eyes still shut, this movement is now accompanied by a rubbing at her front, and a drawing of circles on it, a tongue still forcing from her head ideas and evocations of ideas. Usually it only takes a few minutes to get there, but not this time... now what?

She doesn't feel any relief. She draws a deep breath and wishes that she could smoke, that she could breathe out with each exhalation all the unyielding things within her, the very spectacle of herself in this state. She extends her hand to the light beside her, switches it on, and then takes the packet of cigarettes and the lighter and touches its flame to a cigarette. She almost devours the cigarette with greedy lips, calming her anguish with the cigarette dangling between her upper and lower lips. More composed now, she focuses on breathing the tobacco in and out. She always imagines this scene, but knows absolutely that it will never take place, for she has not, and will not ever try a cigarette. How could she ever dare to acquire something so ostracised in a society like hers, something carved in stone as forbidden - for her and for millions of women like her.

She lets out another breath from her imaginary cigarette; it fills the passageways of her mind with smoke. She lowers her hand to the pillow and says: 'Where are you?'

She is forced to pay heed to her body and this corrupts her vision. She looks for the telephone... aagh... it's always hiding somewhere. She tries to return to the reality that she was acting out before her struggle to find the phone, but fails. She grumbles out loud to herself: 'I *will* go back.'

She closes her eyes and returns to the scene: a faint smile plays upon her face as the phone falls from the bed. Her hand starts to fondle tenderly at her middle, as if it wasn't her. She strokes its slenderness and the softness of a skin that has eluded all the men in this city. She caresses her face and feels in harmony with her body, as if she were two beings united in a fiery crucible. She experiences a rising happiness and is overwhelmed, obliterated, as an indescribable feeling consumes her: she feels her long, exquisite neck, desires herself more and more, moments from that other which she loved as herself. She had valued over the years every centimetre of the priceless sculpture that was her self. This was her most valuable treasure, sculpted by the creator who was inspired to make her. She excelled in preserving what she had learned without altering it by a single gram. For she was 33 and sprawled on her bed like a woman in her twenties still in the first flush of youth: her pores breathing out a hunger for joy – a joy she hadn't pushed to its limits until this moment. This picture above her bed, this drawing of a man for the love of whom she was dying! She thrusts her white breasts violently forward, breasts that she touches now gently, squeezing them between her hands, tracing her finger around the nipples. She writhes on the bed like a child crying on the ground with a yearning for something. She moves from breast to breast, receiving them with her lips, moistening them, reaching out for her heavenly centre, bending her hand to it, drawing a deep breath to take herself heavenwards, sketching lazy circles around her navel, before pouncing on the most sensitive area, rubbing hard and voraciously before switching to her breasts once more, saying: 'Yes. I want you. I want this love which comes from you.'

She rubs vigorously, to the point of burning up, feeling the liquid coming out of her, the thrill subsiding. She tries to breathe slowly before her imagination is interrupted by a sudden stab at her breast, the shuddering sound of the telephone.

A low sound issues from between her teeth and her tongue goes up to the left side of her palate and runs down her canine tooth, accompanied eventually by a faint sound not unlike that of a balloon gently deflating.

She smiles and says: 'You choose *now* to beep?'

She reads the message and puts the phone down next to her, the screen still showing its message.

She raises her hand to her side and performs her usual tightening and relaxing of the skin of her face, rubs her head again, and wishes – with all the pulsating of her overflowing thoughts, Satanic in Gaza – that this time she really could partake in the habit of smoking. She moistens her lips with her tongue, bites her lower lip, then rubs the back of her neck. She brings her knees up to her chest and perches the telephone on them, then starts to scroll through all the messages she has decided to save this month. It is an inner urge that grasps, impels and confuses her into saving the messages of the many acquaintances of hers across the city. She scrolls, trying to reach the first message and to read: *I miss you.*

She reads the second, the third, the fourth... she is counting not just the messages, but the people who have reached her through these messages. She wonders: I should congratulate myself for having so many connections. Or I should praise God that he has blessed me with so great a share of beauty. Maybe I should thank my sports shoes that allow me to keep my body in shape with so much walking everyday. Or perhaps I should thank my mind and all that it has taken in and processed, allowing me to climb from step to step...

And she laughs softly and maliciously... Of course, pride, it is that weight of the mind that drags you each day into the clutches of dark brooding.

She puts the phone down next to her, rises gracefully from the bed and heads for the bathroom. She sheds her clothes and turns on the tap, feeling the water mingle with her soft skin, and considering her own magnificent form. She scrutinises herself in the mirror that stands at the end of the bathtub. She obsesses over her body, like everyone who sees her. She monitors it every day in microscopic detail, its measurements. Examining it now in the mirror as she washes, she establishes from the glass, and the water, everything it needs in terms of exfoliation and moisturising and so on.

She finishes showering as she hears the phone ring and then assembles herself with unaccustomed haste.

'Oh, I'm late...' She throws red lipstick and kohl eyeliner into her handbag, and on her way readies herself to meet him.

With a cursory glance he draws her in from in from off the doorstep and assails her with kisses: 'I missed you... Kiss me.... I missed you...'

She smiles at him and enters the room in the blink of an eye.

The room is dingy, the windows closed and hung with curtains so thick they barely let a single ray of sunlight disturb the gloom. She is swamped by the darkness, mired in her own proud thoughts: why had he made her wait for him? And why had she then made him wait for her?

Smiling, she flicks through her text messages while he gets ready. She conjures up, with the messages, a picture of the man that sent each one, and recalls also what Allah and his messenger said about how each person should not 'forget to pursue his share of the world'.[3] She thinks of all the men and women she's witnessed. She conjures up that girl who delighted in the love of a youth who accompanied her to university gatherings and danced with her. That suitor whose father could perhaps build a flat for him and support him in starting up some business. She conjures up the young man left scarred by love and wallowing in his old desires, until he wakes up from his turmoil. But perhaps lovers have no choice? And she conjures up the religious scholar who teaches renunciation and self-denial, whilst flaunting and showing off his beautiful wife, the likes of whom Allah had never before created, singing of her flirtation and coquetry, her perfume and cosmetics and all the other details which he effused over, and yet crying in the laps of his female students, begging for a kiss. She summons up the young man whom she once saw sitting at a table in a cafe, switching between one girl and the next without knowing which to fall in love with, or which struck him as the most precious treasure.

She turns these images over in her head then bursts out laughing there on the bed:

3. Surat al-Qassas 28:77.

'It is not for stupidity that even past the age of thirty I'm afraid of everything! Of the hymen. Of walking accompanied by one of them in public. Of letting a strand of my hair show in case one of them should stop me in the street, scared of my very eyes, and scream at me to cover up. Or of simply being seen with a male friend in a public place where we might talk about things: What will happen to this little place called Gaza? More to the point, what will happen to us? How we have lost or are wasting our lives, draping ourselves in sins we haven't committed or that we fear committing!'

She feels some of the conflicts rising in her mind, clamouring within her to ask:

'What if I could decide what I wanted? At thirty-three, what do I fear? In five or ten years time I will have used up any wealth I've accumulated, without ever having tried to save anything, or without ever wondering how I might make the most of all those people who practise love, in their own way, on me... Love? That's something we practise without responsibility here, with unrivalled heedlessness.

She remembers all the suitors who once hammered on the door of their house, asking her father if they might approach her. She wonders: 'Could my father ever have thought one day I would surrender to this road leading us down into a soundless, dead quagmire? Maybe it would have pleased him for me to be panting after possessions instead of trying to find a suitable marriage?'

She had almost begun to think about asking for a dowry in order to compensate for the few dunums of land she would get when her father passed on. He died and she was the only one left to inherit. But before she can think too much about that, his voice breaks in: 'Azza, you were late.'

His voice seems to come from far-off: 'I'll just go and freshen up, I'll be with you soon.'

He turns on the tap, and she turns on the flow of all the encounters that brought them together and asks herself: 'Why am I here?'

She hears him humming as he bathes and asks: 'I've been with him for seven years. He's a nice enough guy, a love from the past. So why do I stay with him? Why would I devote all this whiteness to him and no-one else?'

She raises her eyes to the wall and sees the outline of an old painting. Its image is unclear but she can smell some of the dust which lingers on the picture, and she sniffs at the odours emanating from the furniture with which the room is stuffed. She goes back to questioning herself: 'Why am I here?'

She swallows: 'I don't love him… I don't love him. He is a man like all men, so why do I take shelter in his body? What do I get from these moments? Sure, Gaza doesn't give me many choices, I am besieged by its preconceptions and I resist as much as I can this man's penetration: he is a face, a body with the time piling in upon it and transforming it into a soulless lump. How can he make up for the picture on the ceiling above the bed?'

She listens to the sound of the water splashing on his body and she imagines him bathing, shivering in there, cold without her. 'I'm mad. What have I seen in him whilst I've frittered away these years?'

She answers herself – 'I don't love him' – and her words clash with his: 'Why are you still dressed, Azza?'

She raises her eyes to him: 'I've had enough.'

He sits down on the bed, pulling her to him with one hand, positioning her on him and planting an angry kiss on her mouth: 'But I haven't had enough of you, my beauty.'

Eventually, a voice emerges from against his mouth: 'Just listen to me! I've decided. Your time is up.'

He stammers and scowls. 'What are you saying? You can't just call time on this! Nothing happened like this before.'

She laughs mockingly. 'Well, now it's done.' She gazes at him profoundly: 'You'll be like a different person from now on.'

He feels as if he's been slapped on both cheeks and blurts: 'For heaven's sake! I'm supposed to swallow this just because I was a bit late? My love, I tried to get away earlier but folks here go on and on about everything, you can't shut them up...'

She smiles a smile which is more like malice than affection: 'And who said I was lying, sir?'

'"Sir?!"' he exclaims. 'Darling, what happened during the hour I kept you waiting? For as long as I've known you you've never called me "sir".'

'That was in the past.'

'So, I get that perhaps you're tired of me. But trust me, I'm not tired of you. I'm eager for you, every bit of you. Don't provoke me now or you'll learn just how insatiable I am for you...'

She laughs coquettishly: 'Or maybe your wife just doesn't satisfy you?'

At this a grimace shows on his face and he strikes his hands together: 'You know that I haven't been near her since I met you.'

She moves away from him and pretends to sniff. She pulls a packet of cigarettes from his pocket, takes one from it, and gives it to him: 'Let your anger out with this. You're the truest man whose desire I've ever put to the test.'

He tries to draw her to him, whispering: 'You crazy thing. You know the truth.' But she twists free of his grasp angrily, yelling: 'When I say enough, I mean enough.'

He sets down his cigarette next to him, and tries to kiss her with all the violence of his offended manhood. She thrashes in rejection, kicking out with her hands and feet, screaming: 'Mohammed, enough! Enough… Enough!'

He lets her fall from his hands, quite stunned. He fidgets with what is left of his cigarette and mutters: 'I didn't do anything you didn't want me to do. I longed for you passionately. I didn't molest you. I didn't give you cause for anything. In time you will know that I could make you come round...!'

She purses her lips and licks them with her tongue.

'OK, so all of us in Gaza practise adultery in order to avoid scandals. Who doesn't? But do you apply the same rules to your children? You stay with your wife even though you know she treats them like a prison warden. You stay with her although you know she's incapable of washing a cup, and even though your mother starts fights with your wife in front of the whole family. You know that this entire society itself does the same, incarcerates people with the identities it fixes them in, locks them up forever while the cellmates' brains fester with shame and abnormality... Everything that breathes on this earth does this, and in the end they say that we practise… love! You stay with your wife because of your children. Perhaps you're stalling because you can't get your head round the whopping great sum you'd have to pay her if you divorced her? How could you possibly find 10,000 dinars? And your mother practises 'love' because she wants you to divorce your wife and marry someone else. The politicians practise 'love' by acquisition and they are the state and the nation... Tell me, how many can really win over a woman? How many can really deflower this city?'

He stands facing her, draws her to his chest and whispers: 'Calm yourself, calm yourself.'

He seems to have transformed into a different man as he listened to her saying all this. Then he adds: 'Won't you look at me?'

She looks at him with sad, tired eyes: 'Do you want me to stand up in front of everyone and say I want a married man, twelve years older than me? That I am still practising the same stupidity after seven years? This is adultery in their eyes.'

He caresses her shoulder: 'Don't you love me?'

She laughs violently: 'Listen, have I ever once taken anything from you? Or have I spent anything, even if it was a gift from you? Be quiet and listen well: you are like Hell on Earth. Whenever we sin against and injure ourselves we pray for intercession, to obtain a share of the final bliss.'

He mutters and draws her closer: 'Is it not your softness rather than your philosophy that is most lovable about you?'

She raises her tongue to the roof of her mouth and says in a voice laden with flirtation: 'No.'

She revels in his expression as he melts before her, gasping: 'You're killing me. Stop!'

'Don't say, "I love you", say, "I enjoy you." Don't give what you want the name of love.'

'Ach,' he retorts: 'We didn't even have a complete sexual relationship, not even once! What do you want now?'

She draws closer to him, flirting with him through her subtle facial movements, making him melt with each one and swallow his saliva with fear and a desire greater than ever before. She runs her hand up his thigh, raising it to his trouser pocket, drawing out his wallet and taking from it a handful of cash, as he simply stares, astonished. She turns her back.

Placing the wallet on the dresser in front of her, she tilts her face and says to him: 'I have the time now, and you have the money. No-one knows how one spends their money better than anyone else... And remember no hymen can break in a city like this. As you said, an incomplete relationship.'

For she has now decided, in all her anger, that she will be whatever Gaza wants her to be, and *how* it wants her to be. She arrives back at her apartment indifferent to everything. She has lived alone in that big flat since her mother passed away a year ago, her father five years before that. Each of her younger brothers lives with their wives in the storeys above. On entering the apartment she heads straight to the bathroom to wash off the dust of ideas that have crawled out into society through the windows, the walls, the facades...

She emerges dewy, a sea-nymph shaking off drops of water. Picking up the money, she heads for her wardrobe, extends a hand to open one of the cupboard doors, and takes from it a very ordinary-looking box. She opens it with a triumphant smile and removes a bundle of banknotes. This is what is left to her. She picks up the box and the money and heads for her bed... She collapses onto it, satisfied with life: the box beside her, the money in her hand, and her being on the bed facing the ceiling once more: 'No eyes. No nose. No eyebrows. Not even a forehead… Nothing! Just dark shadows above me, lines that no longer gather themselves into forms!'

She smiles and returns to memories of her mother.

'I don't want to.'

'How long are you going to remain in this state? Surely there is something you want to tell me?'

'You do what you have to do. I'll look after myself.'

Her mother never stopped worrying at her. She wishes that she could see her now, understand that at her age she could be treated as a grown-up with no time left for liaisons of the kind her mother dreamt of. 'That train passed, Mama, when my father left me with that legacy of his. And your dreams, they went with you...'

She blots out the thought and instead says to herself: 'Not you, my dear. You united with the city and became part of it. You are now a woman who can do whatever she wants in the name of love.'

She roams through her imaginings, before the ringing of the phone breaks in on them.

'Azza?'

'Yes, go on.'

'Could you give me a little of your time?'

She laughs a loud laugh.

'Don't you mean, "Can I buy a little of your time?"'

She puts down the phone and faces the mirror, spreads out her hair, still dripping, and feels it touching her back, stroking it gently. She takes off her bathrobe and caresses her body. How could she exploit it when there is goodness in it? She picks up her make-up box and takes out her foundation, spreading it on the palm and then massaging it in circles over her white skin rendering it even whiter. She follows it with powder, then draws out a kohl pencil from among the many other things in the wooden box, and opens her eyes wide. Holding the pencil with utmost care, she begins to draw a line under her left eye and then her right. She feels tears welling in them and hurries to find a wet-wipe to remove any trace of dampness that might have already escaped. She sighs a long sigh.

Quickly she pulls herself together and draws two more lines this time along the eyelids, just above the lashes, and finally emphasises the intensity of her eyelashes with mascara. She looks intently at her face then contemplates the red lipsticks, choosing a bright pinkish colour. She twirls it from its case and concentrates on colouring her lips with it, bestowing lustre on their beauty, making her ever more pleasing and desirable to the beholder.

She opens her wardrobe, pulls out the inner drawer and chooses a white camisole and white lace knickers which reveal the smoothness of her thighs and the pinkness in between. She smiles and rummages through the dresses in the cupboard, choosing a long black sleeveless frock, and puts over it a long cloak which reflects a little of the modesty which runs into her heart from the corner of her room. She pulls her footwear from under the bed and chooses a pair of shoes without high heels, puts a scarf on her head, and feels that she is a lady complete in her womanhood, no different from any other virgin in Gaza, or from any woman crying on her bed because she has been forced into marriage, or because her husband is not her beloved or the one she desires. No different from a virgin girl dreaming of the day when she will see the first drops of blood imprinted on the white sheets of her wedding bed. She blows herself a kiss above the heads of all these other women and winks: 'You are even better.'

She takes her phone: 'A car, please.'

She is at the point of leaving the apartment when she

runs back quickly, opens the box, and takes some of the money.

She asks the driver to stop in front of one of the mosques, gives him some of the money and, pointing, asks him to put it in that mosque's collection-box, please. She carries on asking the driver to stop in different places; at each one she gives him some of the cash and says to him: 'Put this in that mosque's box.'

The driver looks at her in the mirror. He tries to hide his curiosity but his eyes give him away.

She smiles at him: 'Thank you, I'll get out here.'

She closes the car door, and heads towards a flat in one of the most beautiful streets in Gaza...

# A White Flower for David


## Ghareeb Asqalani

### Translated by John Peate


-1-

TO STAND FACE to face with death. To choose between two deaths: to kill or see your son killed. In utter terror, I hurled the rock at my brother. It buried itself deep in his forehead and rebounded back out. His gaze fell on me, completely transfixed me. Was he reproaching me? His eyes turned into two lifeless, glass balls. Chilling. My heart thumped. What if he had just lost his sight, but not his life? Had he panicked? Had fear taken hold or bedazzled him? Do people see through the veil at such times, recalling past moments in instants more fleeting than a heartbeat? He stiffened, his finger died on the trigger and he was hauled off into the armoured car. I saw he was unresponsive, motionless. I was a slave to curiosity, despite my fear. He didn't move to wipe away the blood gushing from his forehead, covering his face, flowing into the corner of his mouth. Did his blood still flow warm? I had seen him push the soldier away who had rushed in to rescue him. Was he crazy? Why had he not turned to brutality, like soldiers do? I imagined myself for a moment dying in a heap on the ground, finger on the trigger, inhaling the bullet-lead slaughter in the air in an eye-blink. Yet it had not happened to me and I realised completely that I had actually tended to him with that rock, what with Husam fleeing, soldiers running around and children scattering.

The camp was aflame. We breathed in the carnage and took shelter in the alleys and passageways that struck fear in the soldiers' hearts. Smoke and gunfire thickened. We thirsted, tears streaming. The gas smarted in our eyes, scorched our skin and pricked its very pores. And so the uproar grew, the people pulled together and the troops withdrew. As usual, the people's will won the day. The thick gunfire of the soldiers was interspersed with rocks raining down on the croaking loudhailer that enflamed the crowd's anger: 'Attention! Attention! By order of the military governor…'

I rushed home and screamed: 'Where's Husam?'

Haifa beat at her breast: 'Have they shot my son?'

I kept low to the ground as I scrabbled around the alleys scanning the faces of the children. They leapt about like grasshoppers, taking no notice of the military governor or of anything else, ready for yet another twist in the camp's trials. My little brother Abdallah caught me up:

'What's up with you? Who stole the colour out of your face?'

'It's Husam, Abdallah: he hasn't come home!'

'Well, would any of them go home in all of this?'

'I saw a soldier taking aim at him.'

They'd take the wounded to hospital so, if he'd been hit, the locals would let us know.

Then Abdallah asked: 'Why only worry about Husam at a time like this?'

He spoke as if to confirm my anxiety. Why Husam among all the children? Why David among all the soldiers? Was it fate or war? I found myself melting into the multitude. It was the Intifada.

-2-

'Look! Look!'

Husam lay fast asleep. The day had exhausted him, though a smile still lingered on his lips: something he saw in his dreams. Did David still haunt him in his sleep? Not you, my boy. You're here in my lap and let whatever may be be.

'God, man, I had a gun pointed at my chest. I nearly passed out, I screamed, then thought, *To hell with it!* and escaped between his legs!'

Haifa gasped and said: 'Get some sleep... God give you health!'

She sucked on her lips, her face aglow, and said: 'Tomorrow, you'll be a happy soul again!'

Two reluctant eyes closed. 'Husam is so much like you, Mahmud...'

She buried her head in my chest, breathed me in deeply and slid her hand under my armpit. Her voice was hoarse: 'Boys are little devils. They're 'curfew kids', alright.'

She curled up in my lap. I stared at the tiled roof, through which a catapult shot had smashed a wide hole. Haifa had bunged it up with a piece of nylon. She pinched me, as tears ran down her cheeks, saying: 'Cracking his skull open's getting to you, huh? Well what about Husam?'

I curled around her like a snake. I hid my feelings in her. I sheltered within her and she within me. We became one, we writhed and bathed in the moonlight seeping through the holes in the tiles. The moon glowed brick white and we felt no shame in our nakedness as Husam lay in deep, peaceful sleep.

-3-

The rock had split open a transverse wound in the scalp where it had ricocheted off the skull, spattering blood over his face. They wrapped his head and contacted their commanders to report a soldier wounded in the coastal camp incidents. Meanwhile, David stared back up at them, his rifle lying on the floor of the armoured car. Some boys whooped with joy and made the victory sign as they passed, so the officer lobbed a tear gas canister into the area where all the yelling came from.

The officer asked: 'How was he wounded?'

The soldier, edgy and distraught, chewed on his lips:

'What was it: some kind of picnic?'

In the hospital, the doctor confirmed that the stone had been thrown from very close range and had maybe cracked his skull. He decided to send him for an x-ray.

No mention at all of the events in the camp on the evening news.

-4-

I came back, David. What a difference there was between one visit and the next. The first time, Esther - your bride - was there to celebrate Husam's arrival into the world. And your present was the beautiful mystery of birth. Esther was flying high that day she cradled Husam in his cot. She was captivated by him, swooning over the blackness of his eyes. She caressed his neck and cried out:

'If only we could have a daughter with Arab eyes!'

That day, your mother hugged and kissed you in front of everyone. That day, my little sisters' faces turned red with embarrassment. My father turned away completely so as not to commit the sin of looking on and we laughed out loud. At lunchtime, Esther sat cross-legged on the bed, exposing half of her flesh, nearly making my brother Abdallah pass out. My mother threw her coat over Esther's nakedness, making her burst out laughing. It was Arab shame and fear, something she hadn't expected, but you were typically Hebrew in kidding me about it.

'Next time, Esther, come in trousers.'

And when my mother asked me for your wife's name, 'Esther' was strange to her so she said: 'Thank God her name is a secret.' We nearly drowned in our laughter again.

The secret woman was fascinated, astonishment and curiosity in her eyes as she encountered novelties with the delight of a newborn. She strolled around the camp in the company of Haifa and the other young girls. She bathed her feet in seawater and watched the fishermen. One of the shoreside anglers gave her a fine fish as a gift, which she put in a jug of water. She returned from her stroll with a necklace adorning her chest and shellfish bracelets around her wrists. She chewed on fresh *taboon* bread, a gift from an old woman who had baked it in a clay oven in one corner of the alley. Do you remember that, David?

You said then it was a surprise visit and you promised to repeat it. Meanwhile Esther chewed away at the bread, crying out: 'Fantastic!' She stingily gave you just a crust, which made my mother step in: 'Give him some bread. That's your husband, your love.'

Esther was a child playing, learning, absorbing, bowled over by *taboon* bread, seashells and all the other treasures of the coast. She arrived in clothes revealing half her flesh and went home at the day's end in a *majdalawi*[4] robe - a gift from my mother - and a knitted shawl adorning her head - a gift from Haifa. When I visited you with Haifa and Husam, Esther met us wearing that shawl. There was a ceramic jar in the middle of the lounge, in which she had placed a bouquet of fresh white flowers, circled by a necklace of seashells and bracelets harvested from the beach. Esther embraced the little one and, turning back to David, shouted: 'You look a picture, David!'

Then she kissed Haifa and spoke in Hebrew: 'I dream of a little girl with Arab eyes.'

She translated for Haifa, who said: 'God almighty! They dream of the blackness of our eyes and we dream of their blue eyes and white skin!'

And here I am, back this time and no Esther. Could you ever have imagined this happening? You came to kill me to defend yourself and I threw a rock at you to save Husam. Did you come to make a corpse of Husam, to crush his ribs and tear his limbs while he lay in the bed you once gave him

4. A form of hand-woven cloth traditionally made in the Palestinian village of Al-Majdal, later subsumed into the Israeli city of Ashkelon.

yourself? Could you ever have imagined Esther hugging such a mutilated child to herself, its black eyes extinguished?

-5-

I raced around the camp, rushing headlong with everyone else, my pockets stuffed with stones, racing ahead of men, women and children, while a patrol yelled out: 'After them! After them!' We rushed headlong, preceded by the rocks that competed with their bombs and volleys of lead. I hid away in an alley, studying the faces of the soldiers, looking out for one with a bandaged head. I was consumed with grief. Had his wound been deep? Would we meet again? Would I find the jar with its white flowers in the same old place in the lounge? Would Esther still have the robe, the shawl, the necklace, the bracelets? Do you still remember, David, the incident at the Sheikh Awad shrine?[5]

-6-

A matter for God, Sheikh Awad. We got work for an Israeli construction company. I worked for a contractor putting in residential pipework along the Ashkelon suburban seashore; David was project engineer. He was quiet and meek, came around first thing to put out the excavation warning signs and last thing in the day to record the amounts drilled out and to check the measuring poles. No rest for David. His whole being seemed compassionate, smiling as he did at the workers and resenting it whenever a contractor yelled in their direction. The neighbourhood stretched far and wide in front of the shrine of Sidi Sheikh Awad. Whenever I talked to my father about the project, it seemed to overshadow everything

5. Sheikh Muhammad Hasan Awad was a leading Palestinian religious, political and community figure in the 1930s. He was instrumental in the 1935 fatwa issued by the Palestinian Council of Scholars forbidding the sale of Palestinian land to Jews.

and he would bark out: 'On your head be it!' However, he would quickly relent, recoil into himself and mutter: 'The empty palm can't fight the iron fist.'[6] He performed the *wudu* and profoundly sought his Lord's forgiveness. After the *isha* prayer, he asked me: 'Has the digging reached the big mulberry tree yet?'

The big old mulberry tree stood right on the line we were following so I nodded. He went over to Mother, his mind made up: 'We really have to visit the shrine the day after tomorrow.'

★ ★ ★

My father slept in the shade of the shrine's wall. Abdallah had headed off for the sea, watching the waves breaking over the naked bodies of the Israeli women, while my mother lit a fire under the cooking pot in order to prepare *jarisha*.[7]

At the day's end, the place emptied of its workers. My father surveyed the scene like a hawk. 'Come on!' he cried and shot off like an arrow for the mulberry tree, his gut instinct taking hold of him completely. He prayed heavenward and fell to his knees in supplication, both possessed and humble, while mother stood behind him straight as a spear, her headscarf drooped around her shoulders, revealing two tresses of thick hair around her *kohl*-black eyes. She was a girl again at the end of her days. My father stood up and planted his foot at the mulberry tree's trunk. He took three steps eastward then veered three steps north. He stood in the middle, as if rooted to the spot, and called out to me: 'Come on, dig over here!'

6. The Palestinian expression *'kaffun la tunatahu al-muhriz'* (lit. 'a palm [of the hand] does not strike a reinforced one'), indicates an unequal battle between an unarmed hand and an armed and equipped force.
7. A kind of porridge made with crushed wheat and, often, lentils, among other things.

I hesitated. What if a contractor walked by? What if one of them informed on us? His voice rose again, even more insistently: 'Dig here, boy!'

He threw himself down and started scrabbling away with his scrawny hands. Anxious, I could see the pulsing in his veins. Then, all of a sudden, you turned up, David. What I feared would happen just had. My terror and misgiving spilled out in one breath: 'He's my dad, and she's my mum!'

My father said: 'Tell him I came to honour my pledge!'

I explained this to David: 'My dad buried something special here thirty years ago and came back today to reclaim it.'

David was dumbfounded. He stared now at us, now at the mulberry tree, and then ran off to his vehicle. I was sure he was going to do something and feared for my elderly parents. He soon returned with a shovel, however, which he passed it to me, saying decisively: 'Dig, Mahmud!'

The soil gave way to the shovel and my father's chest rose and fell along with it. The blade then struck something. Father raised his hand and cautiously removed the soil with his hand until what he had buried there appeared to him once again. My mother's tears streamed down her face, while David stood, transfixed. My father took out a small earthenware pot, hugged it to his chest and leaned his back against the trunk of the tree. David approached trying to take it from him, but Father tightened his grip while Mother shrewdly stood between the two of them, silently urging my brother and me to do the same.

David asked: 'What's in it?'

I said, trying to pacify him: 'Well it's not gold for one thing!'

My father pulled out the rag sealing it and put his hand in to feel around for the contents, keeping an eye on us all the while. 'This pot's mine!'

David nodded in agreement. My father took out a piece of paper folded over several times. It was unusually large. 'These are our property deeds, sealed and with the signatures of the witnesses on it.' David nodded again. Then Father pulled out another piece of paper and looked at my mother, full of emotion: 'And this is our marriage certificate, handwritten by dear old Sheikh Mahmud Zaqut.'

My mother trembled, a kindly modesty covering her face. She smiled at David, so he smiled back. My father said: 'These anklets are all that's left of her jewellery and these are the bullets from the gun of mine they confiscated.'

Father then thrust the papers and bullets into his breast pocket and Mother put the anklets around her right leg. It was heading for sundown, the red twilight turning an amazing purple cast upon the yellowy sands of Sheikh Awad, twinkling and glowing. Creatures bathed before their creator and we were submissive.

David whispered, pleadingly: 'Would you give me the jar, *ya sheikh*?'

My father would not let a single tear roll down his cheek. He held out the jar and said:

'Promise me you'll keep your own precious things in it.'

-7-

Dawn drew breath; the waves broke on the sands, the tide swelled in a whisper, cradling the low-lying houses, the souls within enveloped in a delicious numbness. The voice of the *muezzin* rent the skies as heaven's velvet light caressed downcast eyelids. The camp's alleyways welcomed the daylight's newborn as openly as it did the shadows of masked spectres. Slogans, victories and martyrs' memorials decorated the walls and the mass of humanity reckoned up the labour of coming days. No sooner had the buses arrived at the gates of the camp than the market square was packed. The labourers' footsteps dispersed – humble, individual steps heading off, with something new for the hungry mouths that littered the alleyways to taste.

Mahmud carried his provisions home after a long time

away with work. He said to his wife: 'If I'm late, I'll stay over and visit David.' Haifa did not like the idea and a foreboding of betrayal gripped her. Yet she did not speak of her fears, given his wilfulness, though he could read the anxiety in her eyes. A jeep rolled up, its beams slaying dawn's threads. He paled and froze when he heard the order: 'Come here!'

He advanced, seeing men ahead of him and soldiers running in every direction. Kicks, blows and batons rained down; aching bones and suppressed moans. The soldiers hammered them, marked every inch of their bodies, ripped out their very identities, their faces branded with hatred. The breath of morning did not change their appearance. The patrol officer said: 'Put the flags up and wait till we get back.'

One of the labourers said: 'We have to work again, first thing in the morning.'

'Well,' said another, 'what do you expect from the enemy?'

A handsome young lad, who had had a good hiding, said: 'Mercy, of course!' And he burst out laughing, though the pain in his jaw became too much for him. Mahmud touched his moistened face and punched out a curse when he saw the life going out of him. His eyelids lowered to prevent him seeing anymore and his eyes bathed in a lake of tears. The flag fluttered above. A slingshot with two stones still in it hung from the electricity cable, balancing each other's weight. The flag fluttered, celebrating a new day, the prospect of work ending before it was even born.

The sun's threads caressed the alleys and the houses cast out their masses. Children's feet dragged and labourers were ashamed to be seen by such young eyes. A woman prepared long reed spears, measuring out one length against another over her shoulder. The eyes of the workers were on the children; their minds on the soldiers' batons and the likelihood of another drubbing. Their breasts raged. The point of the reed spear went through the weave of the flag and the children cheered: '*With spirit and with blood...*'

One of the men said: 'It's obvious they won't come back to identify us today.'

Another responded: 'We saved a reed spear for the old flag.'

Mahmud's eyes were stung by the glint coming off the flag as he leaned against the wall, a headache raging around his skull and the image of David still roaming his thoughts.

-8-

The new residence stood at the corner of the market. The day it opened the whole neighbourhood thronged onto the first floor. The mayor complained: 'The building's too tall; its windows overlook all the neighbours' houses, Abu Asi!'

The man sucked on his lips: 'Envy, by God, just envy!'

Alas, the original sons of the original sons forced us all out of the eastern and northern districts, leaving us to make do with the west. They wandered around and romped around in the sea breeze. They raised a second floor on Asi's residence and then a third. The building had evidently turned into their outpost in the heart of the camp, an observation post over the camp's pathways. Whenever the camp's mood shifted and the marketplace became a bloody battleground of burning tyres, forward positions and defensive lines, the residence would become a refuge for the soldiers. They would climb it and raise their flag higher than the TV mast over the roof, the roof from which Abu Asi had once lorded it over mere humans. The name of Abu Asi was not so kind on the ear anymore.

In the daytime, soldiers watched from their vantage points over the camp's apertures. The young men gathered together and play-acted, firing guns in reckless showers. The camp was on edge. Storming the residence became a daily hope, a recurring dream cherished in the beds of young and old alike. At night, all went quiet and you could barely make out the roar of the sea over the dreams of the children tucked up in bed, or above the soldier's waking nightmares – the imagined sound of gunfire reaching up to the water tanks and the open-air swimming pool, lying like a mirror to the sky. The houses around the residence received their share of rocks hurled onto their roofs by the soldiers. At curfew, houses were raided and men dragged off to the residence, to be tossed out like rotten garbage with the dawn. The locals would carry them home to their families in silence. Night conspired with daytime, the force of anger churned in their breasts and their visions grew. Turmoil met with turmoil and pushed the crowd onward towards the residence. The slingshots of the young boys; the rocks of the youths; the howling of the walkie-talkies. The camp, the whole camp besieged the building which rained down bullets in return.

Husam screamed: 'Uncle Abdallah!'

Abdallah was a bleeding, crumpled heap. The soldiers surrounded him, preventing the local from reaching him. A young girl threw her body over him, as the batons rained down. Abdallah stared, his vision clouding over as the sand of the street soaked up his gushing blood. It pooled in a great red patch as the UN truck loomed into view. The soldiers dragged the wounded man into the armoured car and set off, while the Red Cross staff busied themselves with tending to the ambulance men.

-9-

Abdallah had disappeared, not be found in any hospital, jail or holding cell. The Red Cross went off and never returned with news. The Red Cross representative pulled at his own hair and screamed in the face of the deputy governor: 'I saw him with my own eyes!'

The deputy governor archly replied: 'We'll look into the matter.'

Silence invaded my father, colonised his thoughts as he wandered the alleyways. Sometimes, he would talk to himself or Abdallah; sometimes he would study the faces of the people passing by, generously bestowing his fatherly gaze upon them. The locals would sympathise: 'God give him patience!'

He would smile for the children as he walked around and around, and only come to rest where Abdallah had been struck down, to rub the grains of sand between his fingers and inhale its aroma. His white beard moistened and shone in the glare of the sun, as he handed out rocks to the children. He would go back home, his glance avoiding Mother's, while she chewed her fingernails and smeared the *kohl* on her eyes. She swore that water would not pass her lips until Abdallah was returned to her, dead or alive.

Sahimah cried, setting off Husam. She whispered: 'Did you see your uncle the moment he fell, my love?' Husam shook his head and looked into the eyes of his grandmother. He shrank down beside her, hushed and overwhelmed. The old woman muttered the Verse of the Throne[8] and ascended to the nightly visions she'd become accustomed to since Abdallah had been hit. Then Husam would wake up, terrified, in the middle of the night, calling out to his uncle.

* * *

The good tidings were like a dream, set off by a passer-by who said: 'Abdallah is alive and doing OK.'

'Who are you, telling me this? Is this really happening? How and where?'

'In Tel Hashomer Hospital.'[9]

'An orchard guard found him and took him to the hospital as a criminal matter. I nearly went crazy. Why I didn't stop to think, myself, when I heard of that stranger found stabbed in an Ashkelon orchard? The investigation as to who did it is still going on.'

8. Verse 255 of the Qur'an's *Surat al-Baqarah* ('Chapter of the Cow').
9. Also known as the Chaim Sheba Medical Center located in the Tel HaShomer area of Ramat Gan. The largest hospital in Israel.

* * *

The doctor said: 'He's rapidly improving and his body is responding well to treatment.'

A man from Khan Yunis in the next bed, waiting for cartilage surgery, said: 'We didn't know his name for a week till he spoke. They thought he was an unlisted soldier who'd been abducted.'

Abdallah was translucent, transparent, Mother and Father's love shining right through him, reflecting back a tender glow. Mother twisted her braids, applied *kohl* to her eyes and straightened like a reed spear. Husam hung around the neck of Abdallah, the two of them whispering and laughing.

Suddenly, Abdallah remembered: 'Esther visited me two days ago!'

The shock had silenced me until I was able to say: 'Go on, Abdallah.'

'She came with David to consult the neurologist.'

Abdullah pointed to a jar with a bouquet of white flowers in it and said: 'Ask after them.'

Mother swore she would find out.

'Did she visit you, Abdallah, her and her Jewish husband?'

She let out a loud and echoing whoop, alarming both the patients and their visitors, all of whom were talking away in different languages. She was radiant with joy at Abdallah's safety. Mother's face turned pink and she signalled to Haifa, setting off a twin ululation, provoking similar responses among the families. They wandered around handing out sweets to everyone. Father muttered to himself: 'If you only knew how Abdallah had been struck down…' Tears welled in his eyes and he did not wipe them away.

## – 10 –

Days of confrontation in-between one strike and another. We sold our souls seeking a day's work, scraping a living from the belly of the unknown. Martyrs fell. Popular unrest grew and the camp's nerves dangled on a thread. These people made things happen; they didn't just carp about their situation. Optimism brought everyone together. Haifa was busy with Husam, who practised his slingshot every day. And, every day, Mother and Father attended on the health of Abdallah.

* * *

David did recover – after a depression that haunted him for months – and the scar remained visible on his forehead despite cosmetic surgery. He refused to answer the baffled questions of his patrol colleague: 'Why didn't you arrest the kid? Why didn't you shoot him?'

Haifa gathered oyster shells to make necklaces and seashells for bracelets, all the while longing to see Esther.

How did the encounter go for you, David, and how did you answer your former colleague's questions?

* * *

I hesitated, my heart beating. Sensations and feelings got mixed up with Haifa's words: 'I am afraid of betrayal.' She rivalled me in appearance as a fulsome dusky bride, in a *majdalawi* robe, her shawl embroidered with determination and confidence, standing in the doorway holding Husam's hand. Husam was between us, as fear for my son took hold of me, but David beat me to it and, kissing the little one, eagerly took us inside. Esther's voice could be made out within: 'Husam! Haifa!'

The two women hugged one another warmly. David ruffled Husam's hair and whispered:

'Amazing!'

I walked around him and kissed him above the wound on his forehead. I felt its pulsing under my lips and I wetted the wound with my spittle. He was calm and I looked into his eyes, surveying for the answers to the questions humming in my head. He, however, looked over at the jar encircled by necklace and bracelets, a bouquet of white lilies within. We were submerged in silence. Meanwhile, Husam explored the house as if he had been born there.

* * *

Esther was wearing the *majdalawi* robe and white scarf. Haifa matched her with bracelets and necklace. They stood next to the jar and Haifa said: 'David's face is a picture!'

She kissed Haifa, a tear rolling down, and whispered: 'I still dream of a baby girl with Arab eyes!'

* * *

I searched for Husam, who was looking out over the balcony, observing a group of soldiers waiting at a bus stop. He looked at me and sighed. I saw him as one great extension of his weapon. He said: 'If only I had a catapult with me…'

My heart pounded. David's scar was still moist. And here was Husam back in my lap, so if he had had his catapult with him…

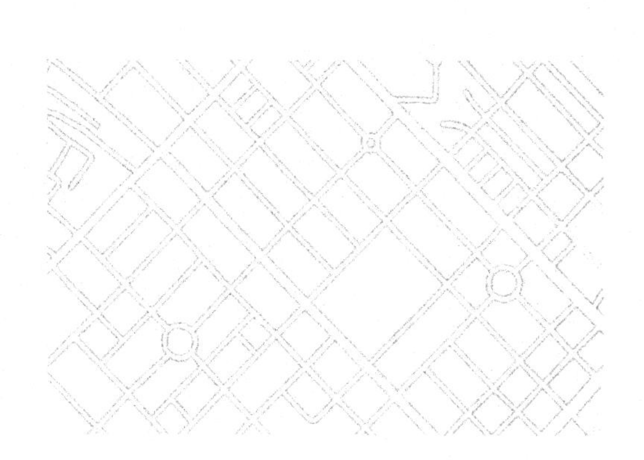

# Dead Numbers

## Yusra al Khatib

### Translated by Emily Danby

FOR THE THOUSANDTH time he read the scrap of paper, then folded it away in his pocket. The numbers written on it were unforgettable to him but, just in case, he had etched them on the wall beside his bed in faint pencil which he could erase quickly should an inquisitive eye come across them.

Each time he opened his wallet the same scrap of paper fell into his hands. He would stare at it keenly, the seven digits dancing before his eyes. Anxious, he would try hopelessly to ignore the numbers. Sometimes they would disappear, but only to return again, staring at him with an intensity belonging to the most shadowy crevices of his consciousness. The numbers would become concentric circles, growing and growing, then vanishing again into a chaos of shapes that could be neither set right nor followed. It was a chaos that taunted him; a memory that he thought had long since dissolved into the folds of time returned to stir up trouble; a mass of dormant questions with no replies, killed by silence as usual. This time, in an act of pure stubbornness he turned against the scrap of paper, a surge of rebellion taking hold. With a firm grip he defied the fear, tearing up the scrap and scattering the numbers. It was their time to vanish into obscurity and remain there; of that he was sure. In an attempt to regain composure, he tried to steady his breathing. What came was a surge of guilt and self-pity for the crime he had obstinately committed against himself.

'How could I be so pig-headed about a bunch of numbers?'

With a quick decision taken by his trembling hand, the fragments of paper were gathered together again, but the action had no power to restore order to this scramble of numbers. He begged them to reveal their sequence and, once they had co-operated, placed them in their correct formation then returned them together carefully to the warmth of his wallet, to nestle close to his heart.

Just one small move of the hand was enough to re-endow the numbers with the meaning that was theirs all those years ago; all he had to do was work his stiff fingers to manipulate the dial, whose ten dead eyes seemed to observe his hesitance. Those eyes were his only audience; they witnessed his restless pacing across the length of that locked room, to which he had fled from a peace-devouring world. Once more he sensed his own unease and closed his eyes to escape that stubborn gaze, and yet it had already worked its way into his imagination. He dragged his heavy feet to bed, to lie down and forget the struggle that had been occupying him all these years.

He flung his weary head onto the pillow. It alone heard the raucous thoughts racing through his mind. Closing his eyes on his recent crime, he called for strength. When he opened them again, his gaze was swimming in a sterile darkness. No sky or stars to lead him in a new orbit; only the ten haunting eyes of the dial. He averted his eyes from the barren ceiling and rested them on the wall, where his attention was drawn towards the faintly sketched numbers. He shut his eyelids before them, anxiety bubbling as the same question played on his mind: 'All this worry for a few useless numbers! Why let them throw you into your own prison for these dead emotions to take control?'

'Put your finger right into those bulging eyes,' said an insistent voice. 'Gouge them out. They're glaring at you; they're set on destroying your peace of mind. You need to confront the memory with courage!'

'Dial the number. Perhaps deep down you're in touch with a world that seems shut off from you now. There's only fear to blame if you can't find your place in the world.'

*Doesn't the world I want at least deserve a chance?* asked a voice deep inside.

*I've never been a coward; I was always one to storm through shut doors, to test my own limits.*

A spiteful voice deep inside jibed at him for his fear. How could he stand there, defenceless before a set of dead numbers? They were the key to a world he had always longed for, one he was afraid would eject him then lock its gates.

Fighting doubt, he contemplated the short distance that stood between his own rationale and the far wall. Then, in the space of an instant, he made up his mind and dragged himself over to the telephone, having apparently forgotten any sense of anxiety for the impending confrontation. With unintended confidence, he reached out a finger and turned the dial. Nothing. He tried the number again several times with the same insistence, making the most of his fool-hardy, irreversible decision. He laughed at himself for his weak memory. How could he have got it wrong? How did he not know it by heart? In his mind, the sequence was but a faint image. He returned to the scrap of paper folded away in his wallet and turned on a light in the gloom. He pored over the numbers that his memory had so recently returned to order and, with almost crazed determination and a single-pointed stare, his defiant hand dialled again. All this for the call to fail once more.

He plunged his index finger into the sockets, as if gouging out the numbers to rid himself of their insistent gaze. Again and again he turned the dial, certain this time that he was not wrong and never had been. He waited, expecting to hear her voice emanating from that other world. Would she recognise him after so long an absence? Would she forgive him for his cowardice and hesitance? Or would she want an apology? What would he say? What sort of a conversation would stretch between them when in the past they had never had much call for small talk? What words could bring them together after the storm of questions had settled and his hesitant replies had scattered into the silence? And then which letters would form the first words of their new beginning? What words held the key that would open the way through to a supposedly forgotten image?

The thought hadn't even occurred to him that she might have forgotten him or deleted him from her memory. She was incapable of change, he was sure of it, and he was the one who knew her best. She would be waiting for him eagerly after all this time, her words animated by the unfaded memory of him. Then a voice on the line caught his attention and he was dumbstruck. The tone had none of her warmth or sweetness; it wasn't her. That moment he had anticipated all his life was gone…

Instead he was sobered suddenly by a mechanical voice that echoed back from the other side of his world. In an iron tone it spoke:

'I'm sorry, the number you have called is not in service. For more information please dial 144.'

# When I Cut Off Gaza's Head

## Mona Abu Sharekh

### Translated by Katharine Halls

THE FIRST DAY:

*Why did loving you not make me see the world in pinkish hues? After I wore your heart and borrowed your eyes, I could see nothing but the cemetery and worms crawling out of children's heads... I write and I feel happy, my pain freeing itself from me, leaving me floating like a lily buoyed on the surface of my hopes. How can you fall from a towering height and not be smashed to pieces? That's what I was looking for when I offered my heart to you, exposed like a fish that had left its sea to live in your water. What were you thinking when you took off your theatre costume and dressed yourself in these little dreams? Did you say, 'She's just a kid. The sea will force her to retreat one day!' Or were you already planning your first kiss, promised to me since the beginning of the catastrophe that is my existence – an existence that has been besieged as much by life as by death.*

Sometimes it can feel like you're being pulled away from reality, temporarily, then you return and the wind douses you in its scent again. What happens with Salwa is different, though, to other women's stories. What kind of woman is she? She doesn't seem like a dreamy girl who spends her days idling on the beach, or a woman frittering her life away on children she sees the future in, or a journalist hunting stories in the street, or even a girl lamenting the loss of her father. Salwa stands on the island of her self amidst a tangle of barbed wire.

Why has she chosen to display her life to me as pieces of a mosaic I have to collect? And why me?

Again, and for the second day, I opened the door to my flat and shooed away the cat who'd been waiting for her food since the morning, to find a folded piece of paper in front of the door, like a sequel to the paragraph I'd received the day before.

The second day:

*Beginnings don't matter much to me.*

What does it mean, that beginnings don't matter to her, and what beginnings is she talking about, and do I now have to wait till tomorrow to understand her beginnings? Maybe the beginnings of transformations in women's lives are all much alike; when I first moved out of my father's house I was a child seeing the blue of the sky for the first time, hiding myself under many layers of fabric. Those layers protected a small, scared, trembling body from the open air that brushed my wine-dark skin and worried my father. Does that seem a fitting start for the only woman in the neighbourhood who doesn't wear a headscarf, and who lets her only daughter travel around Europe alone, without a male member of the family to accompany her?

The third day:

*Today, as I dipped my feet into the mud that separates my father's house from the main road, I remembered the first time I dipped my hand into colour and made the crumbling wall of the house a joyous carnival, and how it had sown surprise in the heart of the UNRWA social researcher who'd come to write her monthly misery report. We're allowed to practice a little rebellion of the soul on the walls of the house. But who can guarantee my father that his green-eyed daughter's joy will go no further than those walls?*

I scanned the letter, folded it and locked the flat door behind me, as I do every day, then looked up to find my sixty-something neighbour standing in front of me, staring, and dragging behind him his niqab-clad daughter, whose face I've never seen. He didn't greet me, but gripped his daughter's hand as he approached, pleading under his breath for God's forgiveness. Why does he come to me when he needs money if I'm filth of Satan's making?

The fourth day:

I woke up, unusually, feeling utterly exhausted, wishing the cat at the front door could let herself in and bring me the letter. Oh and how nice it would be if she could also bring my morning coffee! When you're a woman who's become accustomed to loneliness over the years, things don't always go your way. But even being exhausted and forty years old, and not having a daughter around to make you breakfast, even this has its redeeming qualities. At least I'm not obliged to pull myself together to make breakfast for a husband who spends his nights with friends and mistresses.

What would happen if I allowed myself a holiday today and walked to the beach, ate my breakfast and wrote a little? Or tried to collect together the letters I get from Salwa? Who is this Salwa I receive my morning letters from? I pulled the covers off my body, opened the flat door and snatched up the letter with the fervour of a graduate waiting for a job offer.

*Yes, beginnings don't matter to me. When he came into the shop to buy a feminine gift for who knows who, I sensed the glint of temptation in his eyes I'd waited so long for among my paintings. Because love begins before we encounter it. I scribbled my number on the back of the shop card, slipped it inside the present, and waited.*

I closed the letter, called my manager to give my apologies, and carried my laptop, and my sighs, to the sea. I found it agitated, exactly as it was the day when I cried for a man who carried the burden of an entire city on his back as he left. Events seem peculiar sometimes when we look at them from the distance of a few years. Why did I cry that day? Was it love? When love becomes occasion for uncertainty, that means it's over. And when it's over, we pity ourselves and those we'll love later, for they will only find a subdued, rational heart!

Where has Salwa come from? Who has sent her to dig deep into my soul's wrinkles and my heart's vaulted cellars, opening doors I closed years ago?

The fifth day:

*Apparently, he was well-versed in fuelling hungry girls' illusions. I didn't need that. If he'd looked carefully into my eyes he would have seen that I didn't need all his phone calls, presents or secrets. I was just waiting for his net to wrap around my body. To perform the Dance of the Seven Veils in his embrace, to have Gaza's head cut off and served to me... and it was!*

Gaza, thorn and balm of the soul, whose head I had cut off for me a generation ago and whom I still mourn. If it had grown a new head I would have cut it off again. When my heart became rational I discovered that a true love was always only two poems away from my soul; a soul that stood in wait for its sacrificial offering: Gaza's head. Here it seems as if everything is tainted with the smell of blood and misery – passion in a rational heart is a mythical idea. But I won't let a single kiss escape me, I'll sow and tend it in the palm of my hand like a talisman to give me hope. Who'll tell Salwa she needs an ocean of honesty to bind her love when there's no sacred oath? How will she place her trust on the shoulder of a man who gives his roses to so many women?

The sixth day:

I sat in my office, which I share with a colleague who happens to bear the name of the man who divorced me. We women don't easily forget the smiles of those we've loved, so I thanked God his smile was far removed from the one that first overwhelmed me ten years ago: that one was delicate, transparent, sad, like a child waiting for a mother who's been away too long. In that first encounter, I wanted to stroke his hair and pull him to my chest. I didn't know his name, and I didn't take the trouble to seek out any information about him. Instead I tossed my feelings in fate's face, entrusting it with my lot, and he was brought to me, a year later, as a husband.

I was turning over the letter that had arrived that morning, sniffing it in case I could guess where it had come from. Was Salwa a young woman I knew, or had perhaps met? But I knew so many painters! Did she think she knew enough about me to trust that I'd understand her?

*When I accompanied him to his flat for the first time, I didn't really think. I was carrying inside me a heap of misery, as well as the feeling I could fly, following the success of my first exhibition. Life seemed more generous than I had imagined, perhaps more than it should have been to a girl who lied to half the world, telling them she worked at the university when she only worked at a lingerie shop.*

The seventh day:

For a while I thought about putting a piece of paper in front of the flat door for Salwa to take when she came to deliver her morning letter. But I retreated from the idea of writing to a woman who twirled the pigtails of her soul in a city which saw the bedroom as the only measure of a woman's honour – it seemed like playing truth or dare after years of nakedness.

Some beginnings disguise themselves as endings. Salwa, whose letters kept me company for a whole week, wasn't just bringing me a new story, she was also convening for me a peace summit with the past. Technicolor was reverting to black and white in a film I'd hidden away a long time ago, deliberately forgetting where. She breathed life back into my father, who had made my success a source of shame, woke up my dead mother, who had thought I was under some kind of curse, gave me back a bottle of aftershave bought for a man who had once been my husband, and made me forever certain that only a man who bore both honey and sadness in his eyes could fulfil my destiny. A man who wouldn't leave me except to return laden with passion and love.

*This will be my final letter, and I hope I haven't bothered you. I just wanted to be listened to by a woman with a clear heart, and I think that is what you are.*

*He's gone…*

*He went away and he's never coming back. He went away to get married. I'm not sad, because I never planned to marry him, or anyone else. I couldn't have, if only because getting married and moving away would mean my disabled brother would have to beg in the street, now my father no longer works. I'm not sad he married someone else, I'm sad because I feel cold!*

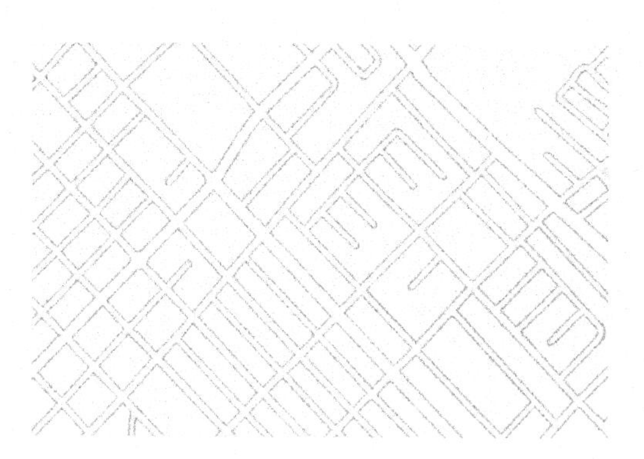

# Two Men

## Abdallah Tayeh

### Translated by Adam Talib

THE BALD MAN'S embroidered collar soaked up the water as it dripped from his forehead. The rain had eased a bit, but not before drenching the man's hands as he was opening the empty cardboard box. The wide empty inside stared back at him like a massive trench. The security guard helped the man place it inside the cardboard box and then took a step back as the man leaned over the box to make absolutely certain it was stable. He could feel its warmth on his hands and against his face, although a chill wind was blowing off the sea and the waves crashed violently against the yellow shore, steadily whipping the wooden boats. He looked into the box, studying its reddish features, peering into its secrets. His eyes took pleasure in what they'd seen.

He felt how soft it was and when he set it down inside the box, it didn't tense, didn't resist, didn't say a word. Stories leapt from its eyes and its secrets slipped calmly, yearningly through. He held on to it after it had turned in on itself. He looked over his shoulder anxiously, and seeing there was no one around, he shut the box. The rain fell more softly as the security guard, standing a little way away, stared at the black clouds that all but concealed the setting sun. The shadow of clouds fell across the sea, turning it from blue to grey. The two men were standing on built-up land overlooking the shore, less than a hundred metres away. As the dark clouds spread across the sky, the bald man stood up and scanned the street;

there was no sign of any pedestrians or passing cars. Drops of moisture floated on the wind and there was a putrid odour wafting in from the sea. The bald man wiped his face dry and gestured to the security guard to help him carry the box. He went up to the box and pressed his cold fingers against it; it shivered gently. Shivering to mean it had surrendered. Their fingers left watery fingerprints where they touched the cardboard. They looked at each other.

'Careful.'

'Be careful when you pick it up.'

They picked the box up as gingerly as they could. The bald man stumbled and the colour drained from his face. 'Gosh, this is heavy! I need a break. I'm not worried about tripping: it's curled up comfortably, at peace with the empty space inside the box. The box isn't that heavy but the air is heavy and damp. It's like it's sucking the energy out of me through my nose. It gets into the lungs and weighs down your breathing. It weighs down your footsteps no matter how careful you are.'

In the light drizzle, the bald man and the security guard withdrew from the square, where they could be seen by any car or pedestrian. The square looked out onto al-Rashid Street and was lined by nothing but barbed wire and the occasional thin, decorative tree that had lost all its leaves and stood there stripped, naked, wrapped only in the wire's embrace.

The men walked toward a rectangular, one-room building in a corner of the courtyard, ever more careful not to miss a step or let an arm slacken, for their burden was heavy and precious.

'It seems like something's moving inside,' the security guard said fearfully.

'It's perfectly content. Don't worry,' the bald man replied.

Drops of water covered every surface. When they reached the door, they set the box down and the security guard went up to unlock it. After opening the door, he returned to help the other man carry the box into the rectangular room where they wouldn't be seen, and where they would wait until it could be transported far away.

The walls were hung with drawings: shells of various sizes, dusty maps of the site and the entire city. Worry seeped in through the cracks in the walls, spreading across the floor, covering everything inside, ensconcing itself on the roof, reaching all the way out into the damp exterior passageway where there were triangles and squares, and other geometric shapes, colourful and intersecting on the floor tiles; peculiar and incomprehensible lines traced over them.

On the rickety table in the centre of the room lay a large seashell that was used as an ashtray; it held some extinguished cigarette butts and the cellophane wrapper of a cigarette pack that had been burnt through with cigarette-shaped holes. The room's only window faced west: it rattled, but it at least allowed the faint light of the setting sun in. Everything occupying that room needed a good wringing-out: the clothes, the hair, the shoes. The whole building needed to be squeezed. Everything except for the minds of the two men, which were weighed down by trepidation. The lightbulb that hung down from the ceiling swayed with the wind.

The security guard reached for the switch, but the bald man caught his hand before he could turn on the light.

'Are you nuts?' he asked. 'Search the place first.'

The guard went outside and walked around the site. When he was certain the coast was clear, he came back inside and raised his finger to the light-switch. Before he turned on the light, the bald man shut the curtain against the void behind the window and after the light had been turned on, he went back to where he'd been standing beside the box. He did so cautiously and timidly – he didn't quite manage to conceal his state of mind– but then the security guard was nervous and impatient and that was even more obvious.

Dust sullied the floor of the room; it stuck effortlessly to everything. Every touch left behind an unmistakable fingerprint. The wind howled outside, shaking the wire fence and the trunks of the decorative trees that were dotted along it. It tore leaves off the trees in the square and blew them round and round in cyclones of dust and droplets toward the east.

The bald man walked to the door and stuck his head out, scanning the street behind the barbed wire.

'What's taking him so long?' he whispered. The guard said nothing. He was holding a heavy, tightly coiled rope.

He looked up at the bald man and said, 'Forget about the door. Put out your cigarette and come help me tie this.'

'It's hardly going to escape.'

A withering look silenced him. He took a deep drag on his cigarette and blew it out hard before it had even managed to fill his lungs. The smoke dispersed in every direction and the bald man put his cigarette out in the dusty seashell on the only table in the room. The lit tip went out and the rest of the cigarette was folded into a pyramid. He grabbed the heavy rope and started wrapping it around the box. Then suddenly he stopped and whispered to the guard:

'Did you hear that?'

The security guard listened for a second and said, 'I don't hear anything. Are you scared or something?'

'No,' the man said emphatically before he resumed binding the box.

The wind howled and the rain was still falling, but it was the roar of the waves that struck their ears and the boats being hurled against the shore.

'There. Done,' the guard said, harried and strained.

'Now it can't get away from me.'

They sat at the table, and the bald man took another cigarette from his pack. As he cupped his hand around the lit match, his body was transformed into a giant ear, listening. He trapped the smoke in his lungs till they almost burst and then released some of it through his nostrils as he tapped his wet shoe against the floor and watched the dancing silhouettes caused by the swinging lightbulb:

*How long must we wait? What unpredictable occurrence is it that stands to ruin everything? The state of expectation begins at birth. Within the very first moments of life, we fall into the expectation trap. From birth onward we're caught up in the fantasy of expectations. We wait for our mother's milk-swollen breasts. We wait to see her nipple. Wait to lie cradled in her embrace. We wait for the warmth and security of the curve of her belly and thighs. And when we get older, we expect success or failure. Life or death. Sadness or bliss. Wealth or poverty. Good or evil. We await every pair of opposites. We don't know which of them will reach us first, and then we simply surrender to a gust of happiness or the cleaver of despair. And we carry on. We bare our teeth or bleed from our wounds, but we carry on. We never have the chance to pause or to think. Constant expectation, and propulsion that cannot cease. Eventually there is no getting away from the continuous expectation of more and more. This is our fate. The fate of all man.*

The wind continued to blow and the clamour of the waves rose with the waves as they battered the rocks on the beach. When the lightning lit up the sea, the white foam floating on the surface of the water appeared black. The spray wiped the moored boats clean of dust, washing them eagerly.

'What's that?'

Suddenly a loud noise interrupted their still waiting. They both listened carefully. It was the sound of a car engine. They both jumped to their feet. The bald man stuck his head outside and looked out toward al-Rashid Street circumspectly. The square stretched out in front of the single room, the rain beat down, the wind howled nearly drowning out the car engine. Everything was howling, but all in a different key. The bald man went out, through the passage, to the bare entrance onto the square. He stopped at the gate and when the driver saw him, he turned off the engine and turned on the light inside the car. The driver, a young, sallow-faced man, looked up at him and asked, his lips almost trembling, his jaw seemingly locked in place: 'Ready?'

The bald man ignored him. 'Open the boot, and wait,' he said coolly.

The bald man turned around and walked back to the room before the other man had a chance to respond and when he got there he asked the guard, 'Is everything ready?'

The guard nodded, silently. He looked up at him and said, 'Come on, help me with this.'

They bent over the box, wrapping their arms around it, and picked it up off the ground. They began moving, circumspectly, terrified they might trip. Neither of them could stand up straight and the bald one began imagining different scenarios as they made their way toward the gate. *It's heavy but there's been no sound from inside the box so far.*

They made their way down the passage, the supple weeds bending beneath their feet as they walked over the old tiles, drawing nearer to the street where there were no pedestrians or cars to be seen. They were relieved and with the final steps over to the other side of the fence they were face to face with the boot of the car, laid open like a grave. They rested the box inside the hollow of the boot, but the driver wasn't able to shut the lid because the box was sticking out. When the driver tried shoving down on the lid, the bald man grabbed him by the shoulders and shouted just as a wave of thunder ripped through the sky from behind the gloomy clouds, drowning out his angry words.

'Are you nuts? Are you trying to crush it?'

'Crush what?'

'The box,' he said after a moment's hesitation.

The bald man's tone caught the driver off guard but he didn't say anything. He didn't really have the chance to as he was trying to make sense of the man's anger. He seemed to realize that the cargo was somehow precious. The guard gestured to them to calm down.

'Give me a second.'

He left them and walked back to the room. He returned a few moments later, carrying a short rope, which he handed to the driver.

'Lower the lid as far as it'll go and then use this to tie it.'

'But then people can see the box,' objected the bald man.

'So what? Did you steal it?' he replied.

'Steal it? What are you talking about?'

'Go on, tie it,' the guard told the driver. 'We're getting soaked out here.'

The driver began tying the boot as the bald man scanned the road surreptitiously so the driver wouldn't notice. The rain continued to fall and lightning lit the sky, illuminating the sea's dark surface. The thunder grew stronger still and lightning lit up the men's faces. After the driver finished tying the boot closed, he got into the car and the security guard went up to the bald man.

'I had no part in any of this,' he whispered.

'I know. I know. This is all on me. Me, not you.'

'I wasn't involved in any way.'

'Don't worry. I did it all myself.'

'Please don't get me involved.'

'Don't worry, trust me.' Then he spoke loud enough to be heard. 'You should get going. You're soaked.'

'You're the one who's soaked.'

The bald man took a deep breath: a breath of rain, and dirt, lightning, thunder, and the fetid sea, and then he got in beside the driver, who started the engine and drove off. The guard watched them from the side of the road; the trunk looked like the maw of a predator coming down on its prey. He watched them as they descended the road until he lost sight of them and then he went back inside, dragging the gate of the wire fence shut behind him. He took a deep breath as he walked down the passage and when he re-entered the room, he closed the door.

That night, the bald man put on his glasses and took the precious ceramic bowl out of the box. He examined it under a bright light, enchanted by its engravings and decorations, and after he'd made certain it was still in excellent condition, he patted it with a loving hand.

# You and I

## Asmaa al-Ghul

### Translated by Alexa Firat

I SET OUT for the university today, knowing the way, and yet not knowing it.

Looking up at the sky, I see an unfamiliar cluster of clouds behind the grey, and stumble, as I always do, on one of the grates to the drain that runs along the side of the street all the way to the end. Our neighbourhood is jam-packed with grates, as it is with school kids, carts selling just about anything, vegetable stands, and a butcher who clings to a dangling sheep as if he were warming it from the bitterly cold wind.

'*Honey mahlabiya... delicious mahlabiya!*'

I move away. As always, I stick close to the school wall, so I don't collide with one of the ramshackle carts, or meet the gaze of those innocent young eyes. I'm used to feeling shy every time I look at the children, whose school wall winds along the western border of our neighbourhood.

My steps become heavy as I watch the children surreptitiously: Over there, that young girl cries feverishly standing over a drain – her money's probably fallen down the grate – anxiously, she tries to slide a thin stick down it, but to no avail; this kid here eats a clementine – his friend tries to snatch a piece, their laughter escalates, bouncing off the clouds above; that other girl there hugs her younger sister with one hand, as if to warm her, while adjusting her ponytail with the other – they stay like that, young and intimate, with their blue shirts and smocks, unchanged no matter how each new year passes.

Minutes later the clamour quietens and I go back to my eternal addiction: counting. I count every contiguous and incidental thing: successive drains (like I'm doing now); the storeys of buildings, their windows, balconies, electricity pylons, the doors of closed shops.

When inside, I count wardrobe doors, tiles, pillows, refrigerator shelves, lecture hall chairs at the university, steps, the geometric shapes adorning my professor's necktie.

I count them all. Then re-count. I enjoy it. I forget and dissolve into forgetfulness. I forget your face, your features, your eyes bound to my soul like a white moth drawn to the beam of a candle.

I remember you. I remember us and those beautiful days. Opportunities, that were no longer lost, because we were together, saying goodbye to what once scared us. Because we were together. The sun rises. Drops of morning dew evaporate taking the pain with them, because we *are* together.

I go back to counting. One step. Two steps. Three. Four.

I forget that you took part in my craziness. Once you counted the continuities with me. You tolerated my chatter, my stories in all of their boring details. You endured my bad habits and irritating ways. Irritating according to you, at least. You tolerated me. Me, myself. My depression, my mistakes, my silence and withdrawal, even from you. And at this point my wound swelled and more blood spilled.

I start counting again; how many times the professor closes his lips while talking.

'Rhetoric teaches us that different forms of the predicate are required for artistic purposes, as well as syntactic ones. Selection of the predicate depends on how one classifies the state of the addressee: unaware, uncertain, denouncing.'

'But, Professor, where is the speaker in terms of the utterance? Isn't it the case that every speaker has an addressee? Doesn't the speaker imagine the existence of an addressee?

Isn't the goal, essentially, to assert one's existence and express one's emotional state?'

'The speaker always assumes deep down that someone will read his words, or hear them. This reader acts as a kind of guardian for all narrative forms.'

I go back to counting. Once. Twice. Thrice. To not forget you. I forget everything. The state of the addressee, the role of the speaker. I need to be this, so that the sky returns, and I can see it clearly, free of any rooftop. But it's all useless. To no avail. You see, the world is the world, even when we, ourselves and our purity, are no longer part of it. Perhaps it's simply dark, with faded features. Our souls are strangers in it, our spirits homeless. But, it's the same world, acting on the sadness of past days and the obscurity of the coming ones, indifferent to the fact that it had come to an end when we had, even if its ending was just for a few moments.

I go back to counting. I forget that I remembered you. I take pleasure and melt away in forgetting. I forget those disparate clouds. The light rain that often brought us to the window. The smell of old dirt. I run through wet streets stretched out like glistening snakes, empty except for cinchona trees, which remind me of the gate of your primary school. Or was it secondary school? The school guard who, you once told me, would rake up its leaves and burn them.

One tree. Two trees. Three trees.

I run. The images rush around me. The numbers get lost. The perfume of the quina lingers in my throat. Petrified rattling remnants.

One drop. Two drops. Even though no water drips from the store awning. Three drops. Four. More cling to me. I watch yellow taxi cabs at the side of the street idling because the army has closed all the checkpoints today. I'm reminded of your daily commute and hours of waiting. All those stories and complaints that the other passengers shared with you, and you with me. I made fun of you (you had ears for hire!). Your stories would pour out: about the man carrying a laptop who opened it, just like that, in front of everyone, in front of the whole world – imagine this kind of technology here, in the middle of a blockade! About the man who wept silently while still managing to tell everyone his story: 'The glass eye my son got after being struck by a bullet fell yesterday on to his schoolbook in front of his classmates.' And about that woman, breathless, carrying her kids everywhere, and insisting on always sitting them between passengers (she was paranoid about the guards).

Nine cars. Ten. The rain dwindles. Fourteen cars. I walk hugging the wall to avoid the puddles. Twenty cars. Twenty one. What is this? When will I have had enough of counting? I've often tried to remember the first time I counted something, but I can't, because of the fog. Going there gives me a headache, especially at that moment when I catch myself doing it, or your finger shoots up in accusation: 'You are counting again, leaving me behind talking to myself.'

Three graves. Six graves.

I'm near my house. This is the only landmark in the area. Twelve graves. Fifteen.

I forget that we too will become numbers. And that there are those, motivated by curiosity – like us that time – who visit the cemetery to check out the most freshly dug graves. I move closer. Perhaps it will be our grave. Perhaps they will like the game, and dig another one for themselves.

Eighteen graves. Twenty one.

How difficult it is to count graves. How cruel we are. And how short is life. Its beginnings – oh, the barren confusion of those beginnings.

One grate. Two grates. Three grates. I've gone back to counting grates, especially the ones you get at that end of streets, near a river. You and I, we love endings. The butcher is getting ready to close his shop for the day. I imagine your response if I whispered to you, 'It looks like he preferred his wife's flesh to that of his sheep.'

School kids move about, leaving behind certain traces of

themselves as if planning to return. Patriotic slogans are plastered on the walls. I think about which ones are better suited for graffiti: narrative slogans or purely rhetorical ones? I hoped that I have shared this question with you before.

I keep counting. One step. Two. Three. I recall there are a lot of similarities between the buildings that we haven't counted yet.

We begin – you and I and counting – to write our story again: I set out for the university today, knowing the way, and yet not knowing it. Looking up at the sky, I see an unfamiliar cluster of clouds behind the grey, and stumble, as I always do, on one of the grates.

# Abu Jaber Goes Back to the Woods

## Zaki al `Ela

### Translated by Max Weiss

THOUGHTS BOUNCE AROUND his head haphazardly. The high beams of his car spread out over the tarmac, chasing away the darkness. He grips the steering wheel with both hands. The sound of the motor growls, as numerous questions and apprehensions churn deep inside. He sinks into his seat. Thoughts swirl around. His appearance: those damn pyjamas. They would be his downfall. No doubt they would notice them, despite the fact that he had smeared them with clumps of mud, scoops of tobacco and engine oil. He takes a deep breath. The road might be open, or then again it might not be. The curfew started at least an hour ago. In his bumbling behaviour he had forgotten to put on regular clothes. Things had happened unexpectedly, at least they had in that moment when the curfew was about to start.

* * *

He had been half-asleep when they knocked at his door. He hadn't left the house all day. Cold, fatigue, no work, and the roof still in need of repair.

One of the group ordered him to drive them out of the camp, suspecting something was afoot that night. Confusion. 'Please, get in. Just a moment.' The car slides along the muddy street. Potholes. Narrow alleyways. Side streets. He dims the lights. Speed bumps. Goes slow. The outskirts of the camp. The western exit. A song plays on the radio:

*O rifle-branch, flowering with fedayeen.*[10]

Sand dunes.

*I have inscribed your name, Mother, on the edge of the rifle.*[11]

'Believe me, uncle Abu Jaber, I was on the run and needed a place to hide. I'd just jumped over the wall of one of those buildings – you know the one I'm talking about – and I knocked on the interior door once I was able to find it. I was afraid that my knocking would be heard, so I hid under the stairs. The staircase alone was big enough to fit an entire house under it, even more. After a little while someone came out, you couldn't tell the difference between the guy's neck and his head. He was as tall as he was wide, well dressed. When he spotted the Kalashnikov, he recoiled. I asked him just to take me to the camp exit. He shook his head, said his was car had broken down. When I saw the state he was in I spat at him. In that moment I thought about wasting him.'

'Ugh. People like that are snakes. All they do is bite and inflict pain.'

Abu Jaber listens carefully. Many things pent up inside his chest catch fire at once:

'Gentlemen, my boy, esteemed company. Trust me on this. Time and again they have dragged us along – on their plantations, in their factories. We're nothing but workhorses to them, dumb as rocks. Anyone who doesn't want to do it can go to hell; he can eat rocks or sand – him and his children. They don't care.'

10. 'Fedayeen' are militants, guerrillas or any group that engages in some kind of armed struggle. The term – which means 'self-sacrificers' or 'redeemers' – is derived from the Arabic term *fida*, meaning sacrifice, redemption or ransom.

11. These are lines from a popular revolutionary song, *`al-ruba`iyyeh* by Sa`id al-Muzayyin, a.k.a. Fata al-Thawra ('the boy of the revolution'). Al-Muzayyin (1935-91), was a teacher, founding member of Fatah and author of many political songs including the Palestinian national anthem, *Fida'i*.

Abu Jaber senses the significance of this moment, overcome by a different sort of joy. In his old age, he would tell whoever was around about the details of that night, embellishing the account with whatever his imagination came up with.

The car stops. Everyone gets out.

★ ★ ★

The way home: hair-pin bends, switchbacks. The main road from the east.

When his wife had asked him what the urgency was, he shuddered as he spoke, the words falling apart. He stammered to tell her that the reason he had to go out at that hour was a medical emergency. She might not have totally believed him, but in this situation he simply couldn't bear to let her anxiety get any worse. The nature of this sudden task required him not to disclose anything: secrecy, to conceal it even from his wife.

His nerves are primed: the main camp entrance. The headlights switched on, the indicator engaged. The car bounds along the unpaved road. Carts are left parked alongside the checkpoint. Pushy soldiers. Nervousness. Braking. The sound of the motor subsides. His heartrate increases. Feels all alone. Would they notice he was still in his pajamas? He inches forward. Harsh lights pierce his eyes; he rubs them with his rough palms. Searching, digging, sifting. They overturn the seats, inspect the trunk, check around the tires.

'Get over here.'

His throat goes dry.

'Take off this wheel.'

Screw them. The words are suspended in his throat. The jack, the hubcap, screwdrivers, wrenches, screws, nuts, wet earth. The car rises up from the front, and he removes the wheel.

'Throw it on the pavement.'

He carries it in his arms, then tosses the wheel on the road like a stray ball.

'Now the next.'

Moments of tension. Unscrew, fasten, unfasten, squeeze.

'The third.'

The third wheel pops off.

The lump in his throat is a boulder lodged inside of him.

'Don't you know about the curfew?'

Throat-clear.

A truncheon lands between his shoulders. He tries to hold his nerve, bites his lip.

'Where were you? Why were you returning to the camp so late?'

'I was coming from Ramallah.'

'Liar. Son of a *puta*. You were with terrorists.'

'No. Not that at all!'

He stops for a few seconds before continuing, his tone disjointed:

'The motor died near Beersheva. I tried to fix it myself. It took forever, and as soon as I was finished I got back on my way. I had to get home, curfew or not. My kids are all alone and I'd never spend a night without them.'

'Well, from now on you'll be spending all your nights without them.'

'This son of a bitch is lying right in our faces.'

'Tell us the truth or we'll skin you.'

'I already told you everything, everything that happened.'

He feels exhausted, suffocated. The answers tumble out of him. The heavy stick slams down on his shoulder again. He wishes he could slap that fat-ass soldier, rip out the hairs of his beard. *You swine, I curse whatever wind brought you here. The metal bars in your hands are what break my back; if not for them I would take care of you myself; if not for them I would beat the shit out of you.*

'ID.'

They scrutinize the information. One of them glares at him coldly.

'We'll write down your name and number.'

*Record whatever you want. That ID is your ID, that number is your number. You can have them if you need them. They're no use to me.*

* * *

Repeated gunfire outside the camp.

The silence is obliterated. Explosion.

The intensity of the bombardment increases. He flings the blanket off his body, rests his elbow on the edge of the pillow, spreads out over his shoulders the old coat that he found in the last bag of donated goods he got his hands on years ago, before the rations were cut. Precaution is a must. That is what past sieges have taught him. He wraps his neck up in a wrinkled *kafiyyeh*. The gunshots come from the west.

The woods. *Rifle-branch*. Kalashnikovs. Believe me, Uncle Abu Jaber. His wife trails after him. Sleeplessness. Mutterings are betrayed by whispers. He buries his face in his hands. The children are all still fast asleep. The gunfire didn't wake them. He prepares himself to hear the megaphone. Long minutes. An hour of bullets and anticipation. The gunfire gets closer, merging with the sound of the loudhailer this time:

'Warning. Warning. Every person between the ages of 16 and 60, report to Abu Rashed Square immediately.'

'Warning. Warning. Every person… 16 and 60, report… Abu Rashed… at once.'

A hail of bullets. The sound ripples over them. The cold pulses with tension. Silence tense with anticipation. The gloom attaches itself to the glow hovering above the cracks in the pavement.

Pleading in his wife's voice:

'There's no rush. Don't go until everyone else does.'

'I have to go sooner or later.'

'Wait a bit, just a little while…'

The remaining words stop in her throat, a squelched whisper slides out:

'Honestly, my heart is tightening up. May God let everything go well today.'

* * *

The tail end of night. Hurrying. Stomping feet, splattered mud, the rain water forging little rivers. Mist tugs at the footsteps. The *kaffiyeh* covers his ears. His chest heaves violently. Faces passing. Everyone heading towards the pit. All roads lead to the pit. Military vehicles chase after the human clusters. To stumble, to be late, means you will be caught by the truncheons.

Shoes fall off and are left behind. Dozens of shoes. There's no time to waste, no time to pick up the errant shoes, bending down would mean a fistful of blows or getting spat on or smacked.

Soldiers block all the paths in every direction. They are kitted out in woolen caps and heavy coats, plastic rain jackets. Revenge fills their heaving chests. Cold pierces everyone's faces, its whipping and bitterness making them flush. The men file into the square. Gunfire fills the air.

There is no time to pick out a place, no space to choose. You sit in water, in the mud. It doesn't matter. What matters is that you sit down, and right away.

The loudhailer spins around. Raindrops collect, clinging to shoulders.

The raindrop has a density that is unfamiliar to those faces. Freezing cold, shivering. The sky thunders. Rain coats people's heads. One of the young men removes his jacket, placing it over the shoulders of an elderly man.

'What brings you out on a day like this, old man.'

The elderly man shudders. Sallow-cheeked, his jaws twitch, and he uses his fingers to tell his story.

'The siege we just endured has finished me. They asked me: "Why are you still in the house?" I told them I'm an old man and I don't have much else to do. They shoved me, and told me when the loudhailer sounds you get out right away, no hanging around.'

The pounding rain grows harder; what falls from the sky breaks on people's necks.

Endless threads of rain roll off the bodies. An icy wind rips through the place. One of the young men pipes up:

'This is an old man. A guy in his condition can't handle this kind of cold. C'mon.'

'*Sheket*.'[12] He curses in Hebrew.

'Hey man. This guy's finished. Look at his face. He's turning blue. Look...'

'*Lekh*....'[13] He shoves him in the chest.

The young man grumbles at anyone who'll listen:

'Looks like they took a real beating...'

The elderly man is like a petrified hunk, a solid mass. Shaking. Constant coughing. The young man lays him down in between them. Abu Jaber takes off his *kaffiyeh*, wrapping the man in it.

A real beating indeed. Black shapes streak across the sky.

One of the men clears his throat:

'My shoes fell off while I was running. I reached down to grab them but a soldier was following me down the alley. He was going to pounce on me. I was cornered. Fruit fell from the carob trees. I told him, "Listen. I swear, if you touch it, I'll bury you and send you to hell." It's a joke, no, a travesty, not a fucking riddle. I don't even know whether that son of a bitch, that motherfucker, understood. All that matters is that he took off.'

12. 'Quiet' in Hebrew.
13. 'Move'.

Minutes stand still. Moments. Time is lightning. Time is thunder. Time is squashed reptiles.

'It's true that if that son of a *puta* had raised a hand I would have smashed him and the metal bar he was hiding behind, no matter what happened.'

The man next to him pulled on the edge of his skullcap trying to turn his ears away before he exclaimed, bitterly:

'What more could they do to us? After all this humiliation there couldn't really be any more…'

Bursts of rain. Bursts of gunfire. The sound of the megaphones growing louder:

'Saleh Ata Abu Jaber. Saleh Ata Abu Jaber.'

He didn't recognize the name at first. Hearing it repeated more than once hit him with a shudder that he tried to hide by outwardly remaining calm. Truncheons beat at his heart. *We'll write down your name and number.* Stinging blows strike him. He gets up. *This son of a whore is lying right to our faces.* The rain pours from all directions. His coat has become a vessel of water, a water tank.

The young men turn towards him:

'Be strong, old man. For sure this is just a big misunderstanding.'

'Honestly, only God is all-powerful. Their metal batons couldn't scare a mouse.'

* * *

The ring road looking down on the pit. Military vehicles. The sounds of walkie-talkies. Trucks, troop convoys. Bulldozers. Commotion, a terrible noise.

'Honestly, man, the helicopters never sleep. They circle all night long.'

'They don't wait around for their wounded. Every one of them is a top priority.'

A faint cry from the direction of the elderly man. He swivels his head, the muscles of his wizened face clench, his breathing becomes more like a snore, spittle collects around the sides of his mouth.

'The guy's had enough, boss. At least prop him against a wall or something.'

Frozen stares. The soldier. A torrent of curses. The megaphone. That sullen tone.

'Saleh Abu Jaber!'

Some women from the camp appear at the barricade, trying to break through. They stream towards the ring road. Several jeeps. A chase. A woman falls down. Some of the covers and blankets they are carrying fall down.

The women try again. They come carrying stones this time. Gunfire. Pursuit.

The loudhailer vehicle stops beside a bulldozer.

'Get over here.'

Tiredness. Exhaustion. A cold wind. A hollowed out tree stump filled with water. Black shapes all around, rifle muzzles.

'Your ID.'

He nods his head, reaches for his inside coat pocket and rummages: a plastic bag, wrappers, the ID card.

'Where were you yesterday?' a rough voice demands.

The coat has turned him into an icepack. He wishes he could take it off. Stillness. His thoughts are raging. The scene doesn't need anything more. It's unbearable.

He cannot bear any more.

'I was late coming home,' he says, straightening up. 'The motor died on me near Beersheva. I tried to fix it.'

'Are you a mechanic?'

'No, but my years of driving have taught me a thing or two.'

Furious stares gnaw at him.

'Where were you coming from?'

'Ramallah.'

'Any passengers?'

'Yes.'

'Tell us their names,' the commanding voice demanded again.

'I don't know any of them.' The reply came ready-made.

'Why don't you know any of them?''' The officer aggressively asked.

He controls his nerves as much as possible before answering.

'A driver doesn't have to know the names of those travelling with him.'

The officer ignores his answer, stroking his jaw.

'Naturally you picked up your haul from the taxi office.'

He senses the trap that's been laid for him.

A car that brings its haul from the office will record its number, reserving a place in the queue.

'No,' he mutters. 'I was in a hurry so I just picked up some passengers on the road.'

'Liar. Son of a whore. Filthy son of a bitch. Son of a...' Fists rained down on him. 'Tell us the truth. Talk or we'll split your head open. We'll crush you, demolish your house.' *My house? Ha. Are there any houses left? The buildings are not even buildings, the houses not even houses, you son of a* puta. 'You were with the terrorists. Son of a dirty bitch,' The blows fall in quick succession. Boots. The screams of the women ring out. 'He claims his car broke down.' Serpentine shapes. The car never broke down, the breakdown is inside our heads, the breakdown is in his family, thc breakdown is among his friends.

The officer barks his orders. The sharpness of the groaning emanating from the square intensifies. The women stream towards the armored vehicles. Gunshots overhead, whizzing just over their heads.

'Start talking. Where were you when the curfew started?!'

Everything they say confirms they know nothing. They don't have any proof.

They got a real beating. He doesn't know whether he'll be able to recount these moments later on. It doesn't matter anyway. There's no need to talk, no need for pleasantries. *May God help you Umm Jaber, assist your children as well. My heart is tightening up.* That part of the woods. Removing the wheel. *Where were you. Why are you late.* Hard labour. The truncheons march on. 'After all this humiliation there couldn't be any more.' *Only God is all-powerful. O, the rifle-branch is flowering.* The woods. That's definitely where the clash took place. Feelings of comfort. 'Tell the truth. We'll crush you.' 'Sheket.' *Shut up. They've always dragged us along. Hard labour alone. It's all the same humiliation.* Words condense in his chest.

He bellows: 'Pimps. Degenerates. Shitheads. Pigs.'

He hides his head in his hands.

*The rifle-branch is flowering.*

Kicking him in the legs. Kicking him again. Shoving him with the butt of his hand. *Their metal batons couldn't scare a mouse.* Got a real beating. A massive blow splits open the skin on his fingers. Truncheons. Fists. Shoes. He shouts through his teeth, his hands dangling. Rain. Stiffness. He makes an extreme effort. A whistle rings out from the square. Thrown stones. Tear gas canisters. Empty cartridges. Punches. All those things hidden deep down inside spring to life: the tips of his fingers twitch. Woods. Clash. Operation. Headquarters. The group.

O Branch. O Uncle Abu Jaber. A tree bursting with water and blood, a trunk made out of water and mud and blood. His stares just hang there. The pitch-blackness grows darker still, spinning. Suffocation.

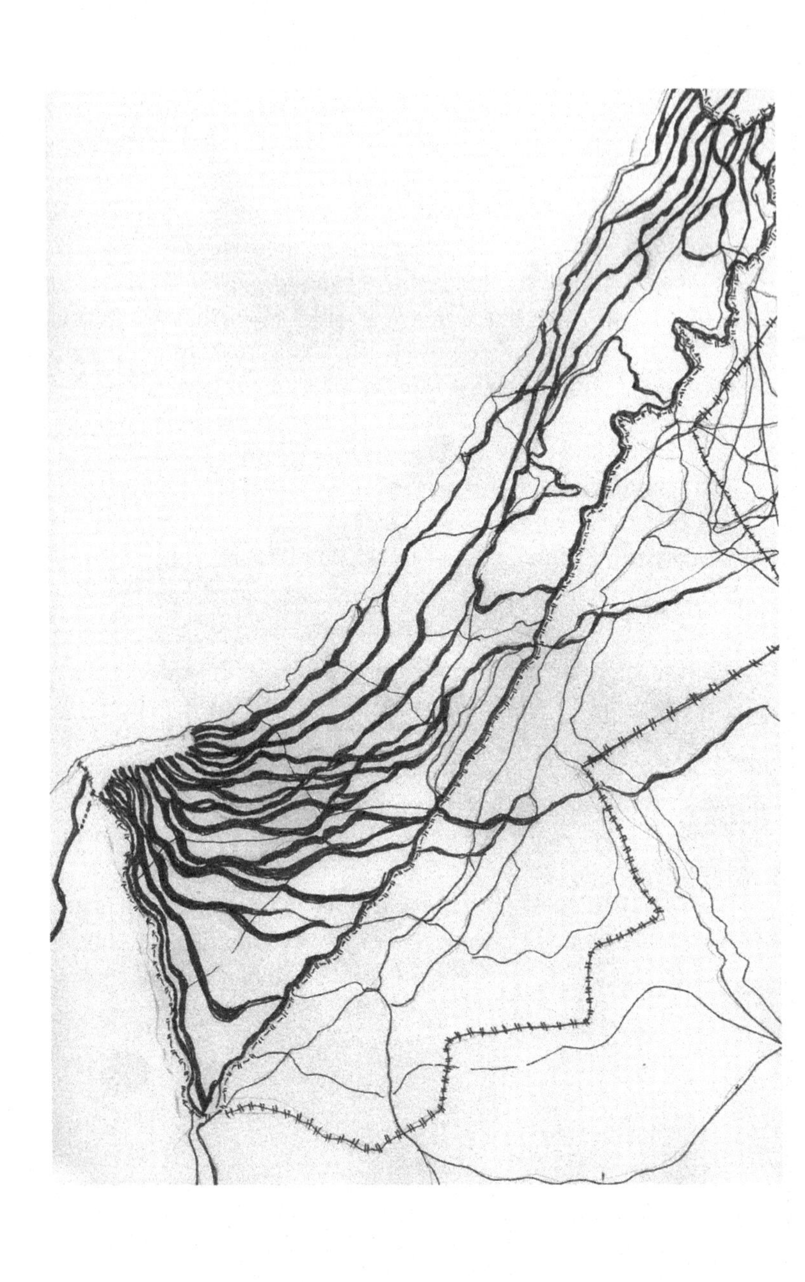

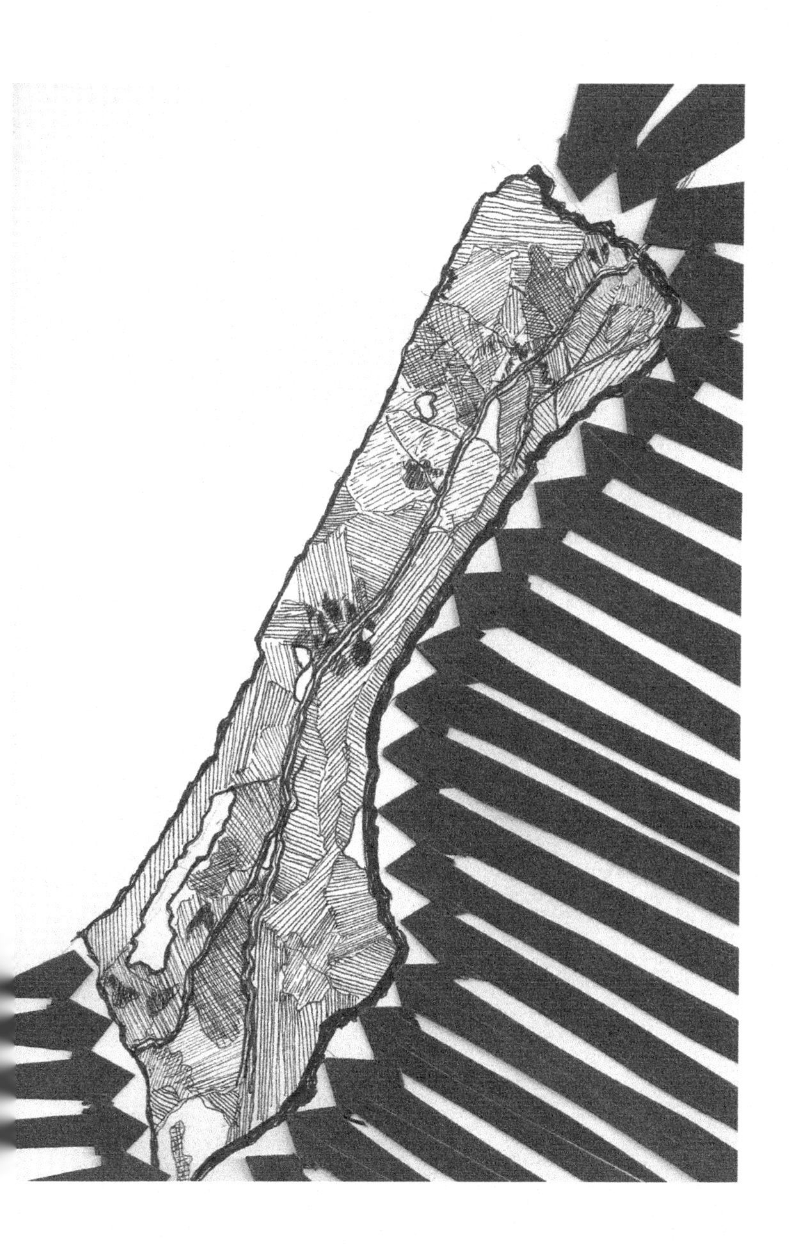

*Janice Hickman*

البحر الأبيض المتوسط
السلاطين
العطاطرة
القرية البدوية
بيت لاهيا
بيت حانون
جباليا
الشاطئ
غزة
أبومدين
النصيرات
البريج
المغازي
دير البلح
مقبولة
شرق المغازي
المكسورة
أبوالعجين
حاجز نحال عوز
حاجز كارني
حجر الديك
حاجز كيسوفيم
القرارة
خانيونس
عبسان
أبوغالي
رفح
مواصي رفح
أبوالحصين
معبر رفح
حاجز صوفا
مطار غزة
محطة مترو
قطاع غزة
الضفة الغربية
المملكة الأردنية الهاشمية
جمهورية مصر العربية
اتجاهات قاطرات المترو
نقطة مشتركة
تجمع كبير
حاجز عسكري - احتلال
نقطة سفر غير فلسطينية
انفاق تجارية - سيناء
وادي - بحر
العطاطرة - خان يونس
المكسورة - مواصي رفح
السلاطين - مقبولة
الكفارنة - مطار غزة


*Mohamed*

# About the Authors

**Ghareeb Asqalani** (whose real name is Ibrahim al-Zand) was born in the village al-Majdal Ashkelon in the south of Palestine in 1947. He has been living in the Gaza Strip with his family since 1948. He studied at the college of Agriculture in the Univsersity of Alexandria in Egypt, and received a degree in (Higher) Education in Islamic Studies in Cairo. He has worked as an agricultural engineer on the Euphrates Dam in Syria, as well as a teacher in the Gaza Strip. He also worked as a director in the Ministry of Culture and a Media spokesperson for the Palestine International Book Fair. He represented Palestine at the Spring Palestinian Culture Fair in 1997, and since 2010 has been Deputy Secretary General to the Palestinian Writers' Union and Chairman of the Gaza branch. He is the author of nine novels, six short story collections, three collections of essays, as well as three collections of stories online. His articles have been published widely across national print media. He was the winner of the short story prize from New Bethlehem University in 1976, and from the Palestinian Writers' Union in 1991. His short stories have been translated into English, French, Spanish and Russian.

**Najlaa Ataallah** was born in 1987 and is a Palestine writer based in Gaza. She has a BA in Architectural Engineering, which she obtained from the Islamic University in Gaza in 2010 and is currently writing a Masters thesis in Engineering Project Management, at the same university. Whilst still in secondary education, she won numerous prizes for her writing including an award for Best Play from the Holest Cultural Centre. She published her first novel *I Loved Her So* at the age of fifteen, and her second novel, *A Cup of Coffee* was published by the Palestinian Ministry of Media. Her Young Adult novel *The Photo* was listed as one of the best 100 books in the Arab world in 2009. Her debut short story collection, *Croke* (2012) was the winner of the Najati Sidqi Competition in Ramallah, presented by the Palestinian Minister of Culture. In 2013 she participated in a short story festival in Morocco, representing Palestine.

**Zaki al 'Ela** (1950-2008) is regarded as one of the fathers of the Gazan short story. Born in the Jabaliya camp, to a family that originated from Yibna, al 'Ela received numerous awards for his short fiction including the Bethlehem University Short Story Prize 1977, and the Palestinian Writers Union's First Prize in 1989. He received a master's in Literature and Criticism from Ain Shams Uni, and a PhD from the Institute of Arab Research and Studies (both in Cairo). He published six collections of short stories – *The Thirst* (1978), *The Mountain Does Not Come* (1980, both with Dar Kitab), *The Heritage of the Palestinian Sea* (Dar Rowad, 1982), *The Walls of Blood* (Ogarit, 1889), *A Period of Absence* (Ogarit, 1998), and *Deep Grey Sea* (Ogarit, 2000) – as well as criticism and non-fiction. He was the Managing Editor of *The Journal of the Word*, and a founding member of the Palestinian Writers Union.

**Asmaa al Ghul** was born in 1982 in Rafah, a Gazan city bordering Egypt whose population is mainly Palestinian refugees. In 2003, she married an Egyptian poet and moved to Abu Dhabi. She and her husband later divorced, and she returned to Gaza with their son. At the age of 18, al Ghul won the Palestinian Youth Literature Award. In 2010, she received a Hellman/Hammett award from Human Rights Watch, aimed at helping writers 'who dare to express ideas that criticize official public policy or people in power.' In 2012, al Ghul was awarded the Courage in Journalism Award by the International Women's Media Foundation. She works for Lebanon's Samir Kassir Foundation, which lobbies for media freedom. Her work has been translated into English, Danish and Korean.

**Yusra al Khatib** is a short story writer and poet and is a member of both the Union of Arab Writers Online and the Palestinian Writers' Union. She was winner of the Creative Woman Award for the best short story in 2014. Her poems and stories have been widely published online, as well as in national and international magazines. Her first short story collection, entitled *Sometimes the Sea is Thirsty*, was published by the Shams Institute for Publishing and Media in Cairo in 2009. Her first collection of prose poetry *As if it Were a Homeland* was published in 2013 by al-Hidhara lil-Nashar in Cairo and she has a forthcoming collection of very short stories under the title *Between Two Brackets with an Asterisk*. She holds a bachelor degree in Administration and Economics and is currently working as a teacher.

**Nayrouz Qarmout** is a Palestinian writer and activist. Born in Damascus in 1984, as a Palestinian refugee, she returned to the Gaza Strip, as part of the 1994 Israeli-Palestinian Peace Agreement, where she now lives. She graduated from al-Azhar University in Gaza with a degree in Economics. She currently works in the Ministry of Women's Affairs, raising awareness of gender issues and promoting the political and economic role of women in policy and law, as well as the defence of women from abuse, and highlighting the role of women's issues in the media. Her political, social and literary articles have appeared in numerous newspapers and magazines, and online. She has also written screenplays for several short films dealing with women's rights. She is a social activist and a member of several youth initiatives, campaigning for social change in Palestine.

**Atef Abu Saif** was born in the Jabaliya refugee camp in the Gaza Strip in 1973. He holds a bachelor's degree from the University of Birzeit and a master's degree from the University of Bradford. Recently, he received his PhD in Political and Social Sciences from the European University Institute in Florence. He is the author of four novels: *Shadows in the Memory* (1997), *The Tale of the Harvest Night* (1999), *Snowball* (2000), and *The Salty Grape of Paradise* (2003 & 2006). He has also published a collection of short stories entitled *Everything is Normal.* Abu Saif is also the author of *Civil Society and the State: Theoretical Perspectives with Particular Reference to Palestine*, published in Amman in 2005. He is a regular contributor to several Palestinian and Arabic newspapers and journals.

**Mona Abu Sharekh**'s family was originally from Ashkelon (her father being expelled from his land in 1948). She studied English Literature at Islamic University of Gaza from 2001 to 2005, then took a Masters degree in Business Administration at the same university. Her first collection of short stories, *What the Madman Said* was published in 2008 by the Palestinian Writers Union, and deals with life in Gaza shortly after the second intifada (2006-2007). She has recently completed her second collection, about Palestinian women, *When I Cut Off the Head of Gaza*, and she is currently working on a novel, about children abandoned for the shame of being born out of wedlock. She has worked as project manager for a number of Palestinian NGOs, and her writing frequently draws on her experiences of social work.

**Talal Abu Shawish** was born in Nuseirat Refugee Camp in 1967, and is currently Assistant Director of the Boys Preparatory School for Refugees in Gaza. He has published three short story collections – *The Rest are Not For Sale*

(2010), *The Assassination of a Painting* (2010) and *Goodbye, Dear Prophets* (2011) – and three novels: *We Deserve a Better Death* (2012), *Middle Eastern Nightmares* (2013), and *Seasons of Love and Blood* (2014). His work has won three awards (the Ministry ofYouth and Sports' Story Competition in 1996 and 1997, and the Italian Sea That Connects Award, 1998). Shawish was President of the Association of New Prospects for Community Development, 2007-2011, and is a member of the Palestinian Writers Union.

**Abdallah Tayeh** is a founding member and Deputy President of the Palestinian Writers' Union and Vice President of the Afro-Asian Writers' Organization in Palestine. His political articles have been published in many Arab publications and he is an editor of the literary magazines *El Zawia* and *Dafater Thagafia*. He has published five collections of short stories: *Who Knocks at the Door* (1997), *The Circles are Orange* (1991), *Searching is a Continuous Rhythm* (1997), *Waves Slipping Away* (2001) and *Soldiers Who Don't Like Butterflies* (2003), as well as five novels: *Those Who Search for the Sun* (1979), *The Car and the Night* (1982), *The Prickly Pear Will Ripen Soon* (1983), *Faces in Hot Water* (1996) and *The Moon in Beit Daras* (2001).

# About the Translators

**Thomas Aplin** was born in England in 1979. He has a first class bachelors degree in Arabic and is currently pursuing a PhD on the Saudi novel at the University of Edinburgh. His love for contemporary Arabic fiction was kindled by the novels of the celebrated author, Abdelrahman Munif, which he read as an undergraduate during a year spent studying in Damascus. In addition to contributing to publications such as *The Caravan, Banipal Magazine* and the International Prize for Arabic Fiction (IPAF), Thomas is involved in a number of cultural projects across the Gulf region. Researching heritage traditions with a hope to promote their preservation, he has a particular interest in Nabati poetry and folktales.

**Charis Bredin** is a PhD student at SOAS with a scholarship from the Wolfson Foundation. Her research looks at animals in modern Libyan fiction. She has translated a number of fiction excerpts for *Banipal Magazine* and several pieces for Darf Publishers. She has a BA in French and Arabic from the University of Oxford and an MA in Arabic Literature from SOAS.

**Emily Danby** is a translator of literary and media Arabic with a particular interest in women's writing and the literature of the Levant. After graduating from Oxford University, Emily became an apprentice on the British Centre for Literary Translation mentorship scheme. Her published works include a translation of Samar Yazbek's *Cinnamon* along with pieces for the BBC, the Guardian, Saqi and Arabia Books.

**Alexa Firat** is an assistant professor of Arabic and Arabic Literature at Temple University in Philadelphia, PA. Her recent translations include the Naguib Mahfouz award-winning novel *Writing Love* by the Syrian novelist Khalil Sweileh. She has translated short stories by Ibrahim Samuel and others, including poetry, that can be found on the Words Without Borders website, and in print in the *Anthology of Saudi Arabian Literature* and *Beirut 39*. She is currently working on a book about Syrian novel-writing practices, and is also working on a research project concerning creative historical narratives in the Levant.

**Alice Guthrie** studied Arabic at Exeter University and IFEAD (now IFPO) in Damascus, graduating in 2008. Since then her translations of Arab authors have been published by Comma, Saqi, World Literature Today and others, as well as in a broad range of online and print media. She is currently Translator in Residence at Free Word Centre, London, where she has been devising and delivering translation workshops for schools and community groups in London and Bristol. Current translation projects include literature by contemporary Syrian writers such as Rasha Abbas and Zaher Omareen, and a series of historical documents from Egypt.

**Katharine Halls** studied Hebrew and Arabic and currently teaches Arabic at the University of Oxford. She holds an MA in translation from the University of Manchester and specialises in literary translation, drama translation and subtitling. She has recently completed a translation, with Adam Talib, of Raja Alem's Booker-prize-winning *The Dove's Necklace.*

**Sarah Irving** is the author of *Leila Khaled: Icon of Palestinian Liberation* (Pluto, 2012) and the *Bradt Guide to Palestine* (Bradt, 2011). With Sharyn Lock she is co-author of *Gaza: Beneath* *the Bombs* (Pluto, 2010) and with Henry Bell, co-editor of *A Bird is Not a Stone*, a collection of contemporary Palestinian poetry translated into the languages of Scotland (Freight, 2014). She teaches Arabic at the University of Edinburgh, where she is researching a PhD in pre-Nakba Palestinian history.

**Elisabeth Jaquette** is a writer and translator. Her translations of Arabic literature have been published in *Banipal* and *Words Without Borders*, and are forthcoming in *Portal 9*. She has worked as a translator for the PEN World Voices Festival, and was the Arabic reading group chair for And Other Stories Publishing. Jaquette was a CASA fellow at the American University in Cairo in 2012–13, and is currently a graduate student at Columbia University.

**John Peate** has degrees in Arabic and English, a Master's in Translation and a PhD in Arabic linguistics. He has taught at the UK Universities of Leeds, Salford and Bangor, is a former BBC journalist and now works as a Middle East analyst. He has had translations of work by more than thirty authors published in *Banipal* magazine, the *Beirut39* anthology, a Saudi short story collection, the journal *Metamorphoses* and for the Rotterdam Poetry Festival, among others.

**Adam Talib** is the translator of Fadi Azzam's *Sarmada*, Khairy Shalaby's *The Hashish Waiter*, and Mekkawi Said's *Cairo Swan Song*. Most recently he co-translated (with Katharine Halls) Raja Alem's *The Dove's Necklace*. He teaches classical Arabic literature at the American University in Cairo.

**Max Weiss** is Elias Boudinot Bicentennial Preceptor and Assistant Professor of History and Near Eastern Studies at Princeton University. He is the author of *In the Shadow of Sectarianism: Law, Shi`ism, and the Making of Modern Lebanon*, and the translator from the Arabic of Samar Yazbek, *A Woman* *in the Crossfire: Diaries of the Syrian Revolution*, and Nihad Sirees, *The Silence and the Roar*. Currently he is translating Mamdouh Azzam, *Ascension to Death*. Ph.D. Stanford University.

# Artist

**Mohamed Abusal** (b. 1976, Gaza) is the creator of *A Metro in Gaza* (see page 118), which proposes a network of seven metro lines connecting different areas of the Strip. The work included an illuminated metro sign which Abusal positioned and photographed in various places where metro stations might, or should be. His project 'Shambar' (2013) explored the challenges of living with Gaza's continual, erratic and deliberately imposed power cuts, and has been shown at Al-Mamal Foundation in Jerusalem, and the French Institute in Gaza, Ramallah, and Nablus. His work has been shown world-wide and in 2005 he was awarded the Charles Aspry Prize for Contemporary Art.
Visit: www.abusalmohamed.com

# Special Thanks

The publisher would like to thank the following, without whom this book would not have been possible: Joumana Haddad, Ewan Stein, Marilyn Booth, Arwa Aburawa, Wasseem El Sarraj, Mohammed Ghalayini, Yasmeen El Khoudary, Robin Yassin-Kassab, Omar Qattan, Rachael Jarvis, Emma Cleave, Hala Salah Eldin, Holly Francis, and Alexandria Brightmore.

ALSO AVAILABLE IN THIS SERIES...

## The Book of Tokyo

978-1905583577

Edited by Michael Emmerich, Matsuie Masashi & Jim Hinks

*Featuring:*

Hiromi Kawakami, Shuichi Yoshida, Toshiyuki Horie, Hideo Furukawa, Kaori Ekuni, Osamu Hashimoto, Banana Yoshimoto, Mitsuyo Kakuta, Nao-Cola Yamazaki & Hitomi Kanehara.

## The Book of Rio

978-1905583683

Edited by Toni Marques & Katie Slade

*Featuring:*

Cesar Cardoso, Joao Gilberto Noll, Domingos Pellegrini, Nei Lopes, Luiz Ruffato, Sergio Sant'Anna, Marcelo Moutinho, Joao Ximenes Braga, Patricia Melo & Elvira Vigna.

## The Book of Istanbul

978-1905583317

Edited by Gul Turner & Jim Hinks

*Featuring:*

Nedim Gursel, Mehmet Zaman Saçlioglu, Muge Iplikci, Murrat Gülsoy, Sema Kaygusuz, Turker Armaner, Özen Yula, Mario Levy, Gönül Kivilcim & Karin Karakasli.

## The Book of Liverpool

978-1905583096

Edited by Maria Crossan & Eleanor Rees

*Featuring:*

Ramsey Campbell, Lucy Ashley, Dinesh Allirajah, Frank Cottrell Boyce, Margaret Murphy, Eleanor Rees, Tracy Aston, Beryl Bainbridge, Paul Farley, James Friel, Clive Barker & Brian Patten.

## The Book of Leeds

978-1905583010

Edited by Maria Crossan & Tom Palmer

*Featuring:*

Martyn Bedford, Jeremy Dyson, Ian Duhig, Andrea Semple, M.Y. Alam, Tom Palmer, Susan Everett, David Peace, Shamshad Khan & Tony Harrison.